Terra!

The alien space ships came roaring in, holding a tight formation. Tiger Ninestein held his fire until the critical moment, then unleashed a barrage of shots, bringing four down in quick succession. His pulse raced. The score on the VDU screen read 738. He was going to beat that record of 749! He waited for the next attack.

Novelisation by

Jack Curtis

Based on an original idea by **Gerry Anderson** and **Christopher Burr**, and a story by **Gerry Anderson**.

Anderson Entertainment
www.anderson-entertainment.co.uk

First published in Great Britain 1984 by Sparrow Books Limited
Second Edition published, in the UK, January 2014

Produced by soundhaven books
www.soundhaven.com
Cover design by Eric Chu, Paranoid Delusions Inc.

Thanks to Donna Bridges, Charles Walker, Peter Greenwood
and Katy Jones.

ISBN: 978-0992869526

British Cataloguing Publication data:
A catalogue record of this book is available from
the British Library
This book is also available as an ebook.

To Lion

Chapter One

They came from the cold depths of space, racing across the void at the speed of light. Six space ships, each of them a pinpoint of light, each with its tracer-trail glowing against the limitless blackness. They might have seemed to be part of the clusters of stars and plane that they passed on their carefully charted course, except for the fact that their passage through the heavens obeyed none of the natural laws of the universe.

They had come from the planet Guk in the galaxy of Alpha Centauri, four and a half light-years from their destination. From the very start of their epic journey, the coordinates of the ships had been fixed on the planet Mars; computer directives had guided them through the vast, icy desert of outer space, keeping them on course for their target. Now their objective was almost in sight. The years of waiting were over. As part of Man's ceaseless exploration of the uncharted territory that surrounds the tiny planet Earth, it would have been a marvellous achievement. But the life-forms that manned the six ships were not of Mankind. And their purpose was not peaceful exploration.

Aboard the craft were beings whose sworn intention was to destroy the earth and all who lived there.

Mars would be their base. From the Red Planet they would launch the attacks that would crush Earth's defences and wipe out Humankind. As the light-speed velocity of the ships brought them closer and closer to their objective, the creatures aboard prepared for their terrible mission: to kill, to annihilate, to destroy.

For those manning the NASA base on Mars, it was just another day, although days on the planet had to be measured more in hours than by the rising and setting of the sun. The base had been established in the year 2020 as a stepping-off point for space expeditions and for those who lived there, the planet had become almost like home. No-one thought of it anymore as the wild frontier. Each day passed normally, with space staff going about their tasks of maintaining the station and feeding information back to Earth.

Of course, there was a defence system, along with a radar-tracking network that would warn of any approach by alien objects. The operators who spent their days gazing at the tracking-screens had seen nothing to be worried about. They were well-trained and observant, but they had seen nothing. And they continued to see nothing – even when the six ships fired their retro-rockets and hovered above the unsuspecting base, like birds of prey hanging motionless above their innocent victims.

For a moment or two, nothing happened. Below, in the NASA base, people went about their business, unaware of the terrible presence suspended above them in the blackness. Then the ships opened fire.

Systematically, and with computer-directed accuracy, the deadly energy bolts streaked across the Martian sky, raking the base with lethal fire. Without protection, the buildings of the space station were a sitting target. Within seconds they began to disintegrate. Vast explosions tore them apart and huge chunks of twisted and torn metal flew about like autumn leaves caught by a hurricane. Still the energy bolts rained down, dealing death and destruction, crashing ceaselessly into the mass of burning debris that had once been laboratories, flight-decks, workshops … homes. Long after the base had been reduced to rubble, the ships maintained their hail of death. Long after there could have been any survivors.

Then, as suddenly as they had begun, the alien ships ceased their firing. A silence hung over the planet - the silence of death. Plumes of smoke rose from the wreckage, as the ships slowly manoeuvred into close formation and flew slowly away from the scene, still keeping parallel to the planet's surface. In a short while, they closed on one another, still holding formation, and locked together to form a vast, multi-shaped structure which then began a slow descent. The ships touched down, still clamped together in one massive unit, and seemed to dig into the surface. A new life form – a new city – had arrived on the planet Mars.

For some time, tracking stations on Earth had been aware of the approach of the Alien Force. There had been no way of predicting when it would reach Mars; no way of knowing whether it was friendly or hostile. Now there was no doubt. Earth observers had watched helplessly as their radar screens transmitted the signals that told of the merciless slaughter that had taken place at the NASA space station.

Once before, a mysterious aggressor had attacked Earth without warning and without apparent reason. Now the enemy had returned. This time, however, it would not be a matter of a random attack to test Earth's defences. This time, the enemy had won the first battle and established a base on nearby Mars ... and clearly meant business! And this time, something else was different-Earth was prepared.

After that first, unexpected attack, a top-level meeting at UN High Command had led to the creation of an elite fighting force. Earth must never be caught napping again. For that reason, a unit had to be set up to defend the world against any aggressor. The leader of such an organization would obviously have to be someone of courage, determination and great skill – someone whose knowledge of military tactics was second to none and whose reputation as a fearless fighter was never in question.

It had not taken much thought on the part of the High Command Officers before they decided to appoint Dr 'Tiger' Ninestein.

Inter-planetary warfare calls for lightning responses and a cool nerve. In Ninestein, the High Command had found a ruthless warrior who could, however, be compassionate in victory. His bravery was beyond question and his military training impeccable. In a tight corner, his laser-fast responses would never fail him. He was a brilliant space-pilot, with experience of both deep-space journeying and in-atmosphere terrestrial manoeuvring. All these factors came together to make Ninestein the top candidate for the job – these, and one other. Ninestein was a clone: one of nine exactly similar beings – replicas in every sense. It was not just that they looked identical, for no matter what the circumstances, their reactions, their decisions, their loyalties and their commands would be the same.

The UN High Command knew that if one Ninestein should happen to be destroyed in action, another could immediately take his place ... and it would be as if nothing had changed.

Ninestein had chosen four others, not clones like himself, but people he trusted to sacrifice everything, even their lives, to keep Earth free. Each had a particular role to play and had been chosen for his or her special talents. As individuals, their skills set them apart from most ordinary people; together, they were a superb fighting force, ready to wage ultimate war on anyone or anything that threatened Earth's security. Aided by ultra-sophisticated space ships and weaponry and with an army of robotic 'zeroids' at their command, they were the most powerful space warfare unit the earth had ever seen. They were the Terrahawks.

And now, at last, the time had come when the Terrahawks would see action. For from their base on Mars, Earth's enemies were hatching their evil plans.

Chapter Two

The house stood in a remote valley, flanked on one side by dense jungle and a distant volcano range on the other. One or two of the volcanoes, it seemed, were still active and wisps of smoke floated lazily into the air from their deep craters. The jungle was dark and silent.

Apart from the house – a large and rather grand building, with huge white columns framing the great door – only two objects stood in the clearing. One was a gigantic statue, more than one hundred feet high. It was in the form of a man who was holding aloft an enormous bowl. The other object was a magnificent tree, tall and sturdy, with massive leaf fronds reaching skywards. It was a peaceful scene. The whole valley basked in the heat of the fierce, South American sun. It was one of many such secret valleys in that part of the world. This one, though, had more secrets than most.

Lieutenant Hiro raised a clenched fist and pointed his signature ring at the tree. The ring emitted a signal – Hiro's 'signature' – that identified him: his electronic password into the Terrahawk base. For the sleepy valley concealed the most scientifically advanced defence HQ on Earth.

If someone – a lost traveller, perhaps – had stumbled across the valley by accident, he would have seen nothing to betray the real purpose behind the tropical scenery. Seeing Lieutenant Hiro standing there, he might have thought that here was someone else who had taken a wrong turning and become stranded between the jungle and the smoking volcanoes. What happened next, though, would have given the innocent onlooker something of a shock.

As the signature bleep connected, a door opened in the trunk of the tree. Inside was an elevator. Hiro advanced and climbed into the elevator; the door closed; the valley was deserted again.

Deep below the surface, Hiro stepped out directly into the Hawknest, the very centre of Ninestein's operational control module. It was the flight-deck of the craft known as the Terrahawk, and the Terrahawk, itself, nestled on the body of the vast Battlehawk which was the flagship of the fleet. Ninestein piloted the mighty Battlehawk from that flight-deck – the nerve-centre of his fighting force. But if necessary, Terrahawk could separate from the bigger ship to fly solo.

As Hiro entered, he saw Ninestein studying a satellite picture on the main console. The young Japanese lieutenant hesitated for a moment or two, watching through the thick lenses of his spectacles, as Dr Ninestein peered at the images on the VDU. Then his curiosity got the better of him. Stepping forward he asked: 'What do you think, Dr Ninestein?' For a second, the commander did not reply. He continued to gaze at the picture of the alien base. Certain tell-tale signs led him to believe the worst. Finally, he looked up and the muscles in his strong jaw tightened. He had made his analysis.

'Well, Hiro,' he answered, 'they're definitely mechanical metamorphs, they're certainly offensive and – as far as I can see – they're preparing to attack.'

Hiro felt his heart quicken. This was what all the training had been for – all the careful planning and preparation. The aliens had returned and they were making ready for hostilities. The moment had come.

Ever since he had been chosen to be part of the Terrahawks force, Hiro's dedication had been one of the unit's greatest assets. He manned the Spacehawk, an enormous ship of great sophistication that patrolled the earth's solar system and was the first line of defence against attack. Although he was very much 'part of the team', Hiro was a lone wolf by nature, happy to pilot his craft through the immense reaches of space, assisted only by his troop of zeroids. On the Spacehawk, Hiro's word was la – w - a law that was carried out by Space Sergeant 101, a zeroid programmed to control the space ship during Hiro's visits to Earth. The only other ‘living’ things aboard were Hiro’s house plants, which he cared for as if they were children. They seemed to thrive in outer space and, at times, appeared to be taking over the entire ship.

Now, hearing the grave words spoken by his commander, Hiro sensed it was time to return to the Spacehawk.

As if reading his thoughts, Ninestein gave him a level look and said, ‘It looks like our first ten-thirty.’

Excitement coursed through Hiro’s veins as he heard Ninestein use the code for stand by for battle-stations. He grinned. ‘Exactly,’ he responded.

As the lieutenant made for the door, Ninestein turned back to the control console and the unwavering picture of the Martian base.

Minutes later, he was sitting at the controls of the Treehawk, the space shuttle that would take him back to his plants and to Space Sergeant 101. Ninestein’s voice, transmitted from the Hawknest, was loud in his ears.

‘Treehawk – you have a ten-fifty.’

‘Hawknest,’ responded Hiro, ‘ten-ten.’

As he spoke, there was a rumble of heavy machinery and daylight began to flood the cockpit as the fronds of the great tree that stood in the valley clearing began to separate and fall away. It was one of the many ingenious disguises that concealed the Terrahawks' launch pads. No-one would have thought that the tree was anything but a tree – not, that is, until they saw it unfolding like an overgrown, upside-down umbrella to reveal the Treehawk slowly ascending from its silo underground.

When the segments of the tree were lying flat, Hiro locked on to his pre-set course and flipped the controls to 'full boost'. At once, the valley was filled with the deafening scream of photon-drive engines at full power. Slowly at first, and then with increasing velocity, the Treehawk climbed into the blue, becoming first a smudge in the sky, then a dot, then a flare of light, until it disappeared, streaking beyond Earth's atmosphere into space. The spokes of the umbrella rose, and it became a tree once more.

With Hiro on his way back to the Spacehawk, Ninestein could relax a little. The satellite picture would let the Doctor know something of what was going on in the Martian base, but Hiro – out there in space – would be his eyes and ears, monitoring any approach towards Earth by the enemy aliens. Even so, he thought to himself, better to have the team on the alert. It would be just as well to have the Hawkwing crew on standby.

Kate Kestrel, like the other members of Terrahawks, lived in quarters a thousand feet below the calm, South American valley. As Ninestein approached her room, he could hear the pounding beat of the New Style rock music. He smiled. Kate spent a lot of her spare time composing and playing her own exciting music. She was, after all, an international singing star. Captain Kestrel was a happy-go lucky type, always ready with a joke – as people sometimes found to their cost. She was also a brilliant flier, cool under pressure, with superb control over the fast-as-lightening Hawkwing.

When he entered her room, Ninestein yelled her name, but Kate could not hear him over the heavy beat. She was engrossed in her music. He waited patiently until she finished the number. When the final notes faded, she swung round from the keyboard of the moog to face him.

'Hi!' She grinned broadly.

'I didn't think you'd heard me.'

'I got your vibes,' said Kate, impishly. 'I take it that the earthquake was Hiro lifting off?'

'Yes,' replied Ninestein. A sudden urgency came into his voice. 'Kate ... the Martians–'

She looked up, suddenly serious herself. 'Martians?' she echoed.

Ninestein shrugged. 'Well, that's what they are now, I suppose. Anyway, the latest satellite picture shows a part of their base breaking away from what appears to be the mother-ship.'

Kate studied his face intently. 'An attack?' There was concern and excitement in her tone. Like the others in the Terrahawks unit, she had spent many months of training in preparation for such an event.

The commander looked at her with a level gaze. Finally he said: 'We're on our first ten-thirty.'

On the Red Planet, the craft that Ninestein had been watching by way of satellite transmission continued its lift-off. Boost-rockets flared, raising clouds of dust from the surface. The first move in the aliens' plan of attack was under way.

Positioned precisely between Mars and Earth, directly on the course an enemy spaceship must take, the Spacehawk revolved slowly in the blackness. Like a shooting star, the Treehawk homed in on the docking-point, fired its retro-rockets, and locked on with pinpoint precision.

As it did so, Hiro's voice could be heard on the mother-ship's tannoy. '101, this is Lieutenant Hiro. I'm docking with the Spacehawk now. See you on the flight deck.'

The metallic voice of the zeroid came back to him: 'Ten-ten,' was the acknowledgement.

A large area of the Spacehawk's flight deck looked a lot like the jungle Lieutenant Hiro had just left. His beloved houseplants had spread alarmingly – in fact they looked as if they were beginning to take over! Not that it would worry Hiro if they did. The plants were his friends and he talked to them as if they were human. It seemed to help them to grow. Before he crossed to the control console, he stopped to say hello to them. Zeroid Space Sergeant 101 bounced onto the flight deck and propelled himself up into his 'perch' – a specially designed pillar of the sort used by all zeroids when they were not on the move.

The zeroids had been named to suit their shape. They were perfect spheres, designed for mobility and adaptability, complex examples of robotic engineering. Each zeroid was programmed for a certain task: some were programmed to be leaders, some to be 'other ranks'. Like all robots, they were incapable of thinking or acting for themselves unless told to do so. They were the servants of mankind. But some of them – just some – seemed to have minds of their own at times.

On top of his perch, looking rather like a steel ninepin, 101 watched Hiro making a tour of his plants.

'Hi, Erica,' said Hiro. (He even had names for them.) 'My, how you've grown.' He moved on.

'Nice to see you, Lantana.' He stroked their leaves as he greeted them. 'Why, Cassandra,' he said, 'you look beautiful.' He turned towards 101. 'You've obviously been talking to them,' he commented approvingly, 'just like I told you.'

'Yes, sir.' Hiro wondered if there were just a trace of boredom in the zeroid's voice. He dismissed the thought.

'Do you know something, 101,' he continued. 'Dr Ninestein's theory is that my plants flourish up here because of the artificial gravity. And when I explain that it's because I talk to them, do you know what he says?'

101 did not stop to compute the answer. 'You're a nut?'

Hiro looked at the robot, curiously. 'Exactly,' he said. 101's mechanical eyes revolved, then crossed in an unmistakeable expression of long-suffering exasperation.

Meanwhile, the alien space ship, silent and menacing, continued its sinister mission, following a direct course towards Earth.

The computer lettering on the VDU read SCORE --- 747--- MAXIMUM TO DATE --- 749. Dr Ninestein was hunched over the console, his face a mask of concentration. At his side sat Captain Mary Falconer, his co-pilot on the Terrahawk flight deck, and co-controller of the giant Battlehawk. Behind him, on his perch, was

Sergeant-major Zero, commander of the zeroid army. They both watched Ninestein as he sat, eyes glued to the screen, manipulating the control-lever of the video-game. On screen, the alien craft zoomed in. Ninestein, juggling the lever with skill, knocked them out one by one.

'Seven hundred and forty-eight,' Ninestein said excitedly. Another electronic ship zipped in over the skyline. The commander zapped it. His voice became tense. 'Seven hundred and forty-nine!' He was one point away from the top score. For a long time, now, he had been trying to beat the video. His greatest ambition was to beat 749. Every day, he played this particular game … and he came so close! Time after time, he came *so* close.

A little cluster of space ships came out of the distance: they were sitting ducks! Ninestein gripped the control-stick. 'I'm going to do it,' he yelled. 'I'm going to *do* it!' Expertly, he lined up his shot, pressed the fire-button, and watched the electronic blip zip across the screen on a collision course with the invader. Less than half a second before it struck, the video-game picture cut out, to be replaced on the console screen by a picture of Lieutenant Hiro. The score didn't register.

Hiro seemed agitated. 'Doctor!' he cried, his voice travelling over endless miles of space. 'I have contact!'

Ninestein looked in despair at Hiro's face. Again, he had failed. Failed to reach the elusive 750. 'I don't believe it,' he moaned. 'I just don't believe it!'

Hiro did not realize what he meant. 'But it's true, Doctor,' he insisted.

At once, Ninestein put the disappointment of losing the game yet again behind him. His face grew serious. He addressed his next remark to Hiro. 'Trajectory Mars to Earth – right?' He knew what the answer would be.

'Exactly,' came Hiro's reply.

Ninestein turned to Mary Falconer. She was tense, waiting for his order. 'Ten-forty?' she asked.

The commander's hands were already activating the communications system. 'Ten-forty,' he confirmed.

Ninestein's words, relayed over a powerful tannoy, even cut through the sounds coming from Kate Kestrel's synthesizer. *'This is central control. I'm calling a ten-forty! Repeat – a ten-forty!'* Accompanying the message was the earsplitting shriek of an electronic alarm.

Within seconds, Kate had put on her flying gear; then she crossed back to her chair and sat down. Her zeroids, which up until that time had been providing an unorthodox form of spot-lighting, knew what to do. Bouncing up to her chair, they attached themselves to it – one to each leg. The door of Kate's room slid open and the zeroid-propelled chair sped towards the Hawkwing launch tunnel.

As Kate made ready, Ninestein was punching information into the onboard computer. A frown flickered across his brow as his fingers went nimbly from button to button. Something was wrong. Things were not quite proceeding as they should; and neither the computer, nor their first line of defence, Lieutenant Hiro, could provide a reason.

Mary Falconer had taken over the VDU console in order to communicate with Hiro. Mary's ability to keep her nerve in an emergency was just one of the qualities that suited her to the Terrahawks squad; another was her highly developed instinct for danger – a sort of sixth sense. She spoke to Hiro, now, in a voice that displayed calm control. But at the back of her brain, there were unmistakeable signals that spelt *Danger*.

She looked at Hiro's young, eager face on the VDU, his eyes intense behind the horn-rimmed glasses. ‘Hiro,’ she said, ‘we have all your onboard computer data. Do you have a visual sighting yet?’

Hiro turned to 101, who was nearby on his perch. 'Anything?'

101 knew that the question was more to satisfy Terrahawk HQ than anything else. He would have reported a sighting to Hiro at once, and there was no way that the zeroids would have missed the alien ship. Nevertheless, like any good robot, he took the lead from his human master. 'I'll check again, Sir,' he replied, and immediately communicated with his troops.

'This is Space Sergeant 101. This is 101 calling Zeroids one to a hundred … .'

Along the superstructure of the Spacehawk was a line of portholes. In each a zeroid was positioned, the mechanical eyes of the craft, and each ready to bring into play the inbuilt weapon that was a vital part of zeroid armoury. At 101's command, they once again scanned the space sky. And once again, they had nothing to report.

In the Hawknest, Ninestein looked up from his computer and turned anxiously to Mary Falconer. 'They *must* have a visual sighting by now,' he exclaimed. Like Mary, he could feel that something was wrong. Each data-feed was indicating near-disaster. But until clear kill-coordinates had appeared, letting Tiger engage radar sightings, his apprehensive ground-base stood powerless. If galactic signals were registering on the computer, then surely Hiro and his zeroids must be able to see the approaching space ship.

Captain Falconer shook her head. 'According to the sensors – yes, they should have a sighting. But a hundred zeroids report "no" – and a hundred zeroids can't be wrong.'

Ninestein looked thoughtful. 'Neither can our sensors,' he reminded her. And the energy-source he had been tracking still showed up clearly on the VDU. Tiger made his decision. 'Hiro,' he ordered, 'lock onto that energy-source and blast it.' And hang the consequences, he thought.

As if reading his mind, Hiro replied, 'But Doctor – how do we know they're hostile? I mean, just because they're alien, it doesn't have to mean they're hostile … .'

Ninestein was resolute. He believed that his sense of danger, and Mary's too, could not be wrong. He repeated the command. But still Hiro hesitated. 'But we don't even have a radar echo,' he warned.

'I'm aware of that.' Tiger's mind was made up. 'Now – open fire!'

Hiro gave the order. From the hull of the great ship, the zeroids pinpointed the energy-source and delivered a massive broadside: the full and terrible fire power of the Spacehawk. At once, the sky was lit by gigantic detonations. Billows of flame, orange and white, flashed in the utter darkness, as if a thousand volcanoes were erupting at the same time. Watching from an observation port on the flight-deck, Hiro saw the zeroids unleash stream after stream of high energy bolts. Nothing, he thought, could survive *that.*

He turned to 101, and was about to give an instruction, but the space. sergeant was ahead of him a hatch was opening in the zeroid's casing, to allow a cable to snake out and plug into the flight-deck computer. There was a tiny pause; then l0l's spherical eyes revolved in amazement. 'It's through, Captain!' There was no denying the information he was getting from the computer. 'It's through – and it's heading for Earth!'

For a moment, Hiro stood gaping in disbelief. But he knew that the robot could not be mistaken. Recovering himself, he established voice-contact with Hawknest in order to give his commander the bad, the unbelievably bad news.

Ninestein's worst fears were· realized. All along, he had suspected that there was something very different – terrifyingly different – about the alien ship. Well, now he knew it. The craft had somehow managed to get past Hiro and the awesome kill capacity of Spacehawk. And it was on a direct course for Earth. *Okay,* he thought, *they've got behind our first line of defence – time to try something else. Let's see what Hawkwing can do.*

Unlike the bigger ships in the Terrahawks fleet, Hawkwing was designed for both great speed and enormous manoeuvrability. It resembled a single slender delta-wing, under which was slung the 'egg' – Kate Kestrel's control cabin. On top of the wing, was a small, dome-shaped structure. This housed the fifth member of the Unit – Lieutenant Hawkeye, the gunnery officer. From this 'blister' on the wing, Hawkeye controlled the high-energy laser cannon and guided energy bolts that could bring instant destruction to any foe.

Both Kate and Hawkeye were aboard, waiting for instructions. Since they were out of sight of one another, Kate ran through the usual safety procedure. 'Hawkeye,' she said, after activating the ship's communications system, 'are you on the wing?'

'I sure am, Ma'am,' came the reply.

Kate grinned to herself. Hawkeye's voice was cheerful, as always. He sounded as if he were more than ready for a scrap. It was typical of the dare-devil Hawkeye to be itching to get out there and face the enemy. *I'm glad,* thought Kate, *that he's on my side, not theirs.*

Suddenly, Ninestein's voice was loud in the cabin. 'You have a ten-fifty,' he advised.

Kate began to wind up the engines. 'Ten-ten,' she replied. The Hawkwing released itself from its restraining-damps and began to accelerate along the launch tunnel. As the craft gathered speed, the whine of the photon-drive grew in intensity, until the noise was all but deafening. Kate switched to full power. The Hawkwing screamed down the dark shaft of the tunnel.

On the surface, the calm waters of a large lake began to make a slow, mysterious circular movement at the centre. Then the motion became increasingly violent, swirling and swirling faster and ever faster, until the water began to form a vast whirlpool. The action was caused by a giant turbine, which would create a vortex in the lake at the point of Hawkwing's exit. As the turbine increased its power, so the centrifugal force piled the waters back, until a tunnel in the lake met the tunnel along which Hawkwing travelled at 750 feet per second.

The timing was critical. Flying under computer control, the sleek craft emerged from its curving flight-shaft underground through the automatically opening doors, just as the vortex was fully formed, and roared out of the lake. As soon as it was clear, the turbine shut down and the waters closed. Where, a second or two before, there had been churning turbulence, there was now only the placid, glassy surface of the lake. As Hawkwing flew into the stratosphere, its wing-tips swung up to their operational flying positions. Kate and Hawkeye were truly on the wing.

‘Airborne,’ Kate reported. Ninestein was busy at the VDU, so Mary Falconer took over the base-to-ship contact.

‘Ten-ten,’ she said. Then: ‘Energy-source approaching ... ionosphere at Mach 6 ... it’s a controlled descent.’

‘Still no radar echo.’ Kate sounded puzzled.

‘No, Kate … .’ Mary hazarded a guess. ‘It may be a Stealth,’ she suggested. That would be nothing new. Stealths were designed to absorb, not reflect, radar impulses.

Tiger Ninestein looked up from the console, where he had been busily computing the new position of the mysterious invader. He cut into Mary's transmission. ‘I don’t think so,’ he said.

‘Kate, I’m going to pass coordinates to your onboard computer. Then I want you to blast the whole area. You can't use guided missiles – there's nothing to lock on to.’ If he had not been certain before, Ninestein was now positive that the energy-source – whatever it was – could be assumed to be evil ... and very powerful.

Kate detected the seriousness in his tone. Both she and Hawkeye made ready for action. ‘Ten-ten.’ Her response to Tiger's instructions came loud and clear.

Turning to Mary Falconer, Ninestein said, ‘Use the radio telescope, Mary.’

‘Right.’ She began to manipulate the remote control and a thousand feet above, the huge statue of the man holding the bowl began to rotate – the Terrahawk's radio telescope searching the skies for the enemy. It found its objective and the information was relayed to the Hawknest. Mary quickly fed the electronic message into the master computer and spoke to Hawkwing on the open communications channel.

'All right, Kate – here come the coordinates, fresh from the rose garden.'

Despite the tension, Kate Kestrel smiled. The 'statue' stood in a beautiful, flourishing garden of red, yellow and white roses. She responded to Mary's joke with one of her own. 'Thanks,' she said, 'I'm on the scent.' Then, in a more serious tone: 'Hawkeye – over to you.'

In the gun-bay, Hawkeye grinned with the sheer pleasure of being in action, though he had appreciated the swapping of jokes between Mary and Kate. *Okay,* he thought, *Kate's on the scent ... let's see if I can go in for the kill.* Out loud, he said, 'Ten-ten.' Then, glancing down at the coordinates, 'Left three degrees ... hold her steady––'

He opened fire, letting loose with the energy cannon. Brilliant flashes of pure light screamed across the sky, but they were aimed (or so it seemed) at nothing. Below, in the egg of the cockpit, Kate was bathed in a pulsing red light as the energy cannon blasted away just above her head. She had to shout to make herself heard above the booming of Hawkeye's weapon. 'Still no visual contact.'

'Keep firing,' was Ninestein's crisp reply.

'Ten-ten,' Hawkeye responded.

Ninestein waited impatiently for a report of a strike. Surely the Hawkwing must hit something. Its cannon was locked onto the energy-source; Hawkeye – true to his name – never missed; and bolt after bolt was being poured onto the target. But nothing. His concern grew. Finally, the sound of firing ceased.

'Anything?' Tiger asked anxiously.

Hawkeye's tone of exasperation told the story. 'I fired at nothing,' he said, 'and guess what I hit?'

Now Ninestein was seriously worried. He tried not to let it show. 'Okay, Kate,' his voice was level. 'Stay in that area-I might need you.'

Kate peeled off, preparing to circle until fresh instructions came through. 'Ten-ten,' she acknowledged. 'We'll maintain our present ten-twenty.'

Mary Falconer had been continuing to monitor the progress of the invader. Now she turned to Ninestein with a worried frown. 'Energy-source now entered Earth's atmosphere,' she told him.

It's time, thought Tiger, *to use other resources.* He swivelled in his chair to address the zeroid that sat on a perch nearby, Sergeant-major Zero, the zeroid commander and the sole surviving example of the zeroid prototype. Zero was an invaluable part of the Terrahawks operation: a robot of outstanding merit. Even so, there were times when Dr Ninestein wondered about the zeroid leader. For one thing, robots were not supposed to be able to think for themselves. Their sole duty was to obey – to follow orders exactly at all times. And on occasions, there was something oddly independent about Sergeant-major Zero. It was almost as if the zeroid had a mind of his own; and even sometimes *feelings.*

Tiger dismissed these thoughts from his mind. Right now he required some hard facts. He asked, 'What's the projected landing-site?'

Zero activated a series of pinpoint lights on the console panel, working by remote control. The last light in the row illuminated a spot on Zero's own computer-panel. 'A hundred miles due north of Bangkok, Sir,' came the response. Then: 'Might I suggest ... .'

Ninestein cut in angrily. This annoying ability to come up with ideas of his own was what troubled him about Zero. 'No you might not!' he snapped.

'Reason is not in your sphere.' The sphere-shaped robot stayed silent; but his silence seemed somehow resentful.

‘Bangkok?’ Mary's question was also a request. She sensed it was time she put her zeroids into action.

‘Mary,’ said Ninestein, detecting the eagerness in her voice, ‘it’s all yours.’

At once, Mary turned to the sergeant-major. Captain Falconer was a very pretty woman; and could there have been … no, it wasn't possible … a glint of admiration in the robot’s mechanical eyes as he looked at her?

‘Sergeant-major, I want a hundred of your men to be boarded immediately.’

‘Yes, Captain.’ Zero responded at once, bouncing down from his perch and making for the door. But on his way, he paused and asked: ‘You don't really think of us as men, do you?’ Something in his tone suggested that the Captain might – just might – feel that way.

Ninestein's anger erupted. The last thing he needed in the middle of a crisis, was the sergeant-major wasting time on sentimental ideas. ‘For God’s *sake,* Zero, not now!’ he bellowed. Without another word, the robot rolled across the floor to the zeroidoor and disappeared.

Within a minute, he had made his way to the barracks: a series of channels, each holding zeroids, like bowls in a bowling-alley. Above the channels was a narrow balcony. A zeroidoor opened to admit the sergeant-major, who rolled along to a central position so that he could address his troops. He paused dramatically for a moment. The ranks of zeroids looked up at him in eager anticipation. Then he gave the command they had been waiting for: 'All right, men - let's be having you. *This is it!'*

As the troops started to move out, making for the boarding-point, Zero returned to the Hawknest, and propelled himself back to his perch. To Mary, he said, 'All equipment and … *men* ... aboard Captain.'

Mary smiled to herself. Unlike Ninestein, she had a soft spot for the zeroid. But all she said was, 'Thank you, Sergeant-major.' Like Ninestein, she had strapped herself in, ready for flight. She checked that all systems were go, then: 'Stand by for lift-off.

Two hatches opened in Zero's spherical armour, and stabilizers, with suckers attached, locked onto the instrument panel. 'Ready for lift-off,' he echoed. A deep rumble of powerful motors could be heard and the coloured panels that formed the walls of the Hawknest slowly cleared and became transparent. The wall of the launch-shaft was visible just beyond them. The Hawknest had taken on its true identity. It was the flight deck of the Terrahawk, the nerve-centre of Ninestein's operation. From this flight deck, he controlled the massive Battlehawk: the flagship. But, if necessary, the

Terrahawk could detach itself from the mother-ship and fly solo, seeking out those vantage-points from which Ninestein could direct his forces.

Slowly, the Battlehawk, with the Terrahawk nestling on its back, lifted its nose until the whole structure was standing vertically. Then, with a deafening roar, began to accelerate up the shaft. Above, there was a sound like distant thunder, growing all the time; the earth trembled; and then, just when it seemed that the Battlehawk might be going to tear through the earth's crust, the White House seemed to fall apart, like a house of cards. First, the roof was jacked open, coming upwards on hinges. Next, the four walls folded outwards, splaying wide like massive jaws. And then the Battlehawk burst from the centre, climbing skywards. When it was clear, the White House reassembled itself; and, within minutes, it once again became an elegant, innocent-looking house in a peaceful valley, somewhere in South America.

As soon as it had gained the correct altitude, the Battlehawk flattened out for horizontal flight. Ninestein opened the communications channel. 'Katie,' he ordered, 'bring the Hawkwing to the battle-zone. We'll need air cover.'

Kate Kestrel broke out of the stacking-circuit she had been flying and turned her craft onto a new flight path. 'We're on our way.'

Tiger's next command was to the Spacehawk. He realized he would need someone to keep an eye on developments when the enemy was engaged. 'Hiro, move into geo-stationary orbit. I want you to oversee the battle-zone.'

Hiro plotted a new course. 'Ten-ten,' he replied. There was an edge of excitement in his voice that communicated itself to 101.

'Looks like this is it, Sir,' the zeroid remarked.

'Exactly!' The lieutenant glanced up, grinning.

'You mean,' said 101, displaying a robot's sense of correctness, 'exact*l*y.'

Hiro nodded. 'Exactly,' he agreed.

101's eyes crossed in exasperation.

Closer to the earth's surface, the Battlehawk, its photon-drive engines at full thrust, hurtled towards the location of the energy-source. The atmosphere aboard was tense.

Sitting at the controls, Mary Falconer felt elated and apprehensive at the same time. The Terrahawks had trained for this moment; the endless preparation, the countless hours of flying time, the days spent studying new computer technology and learning to act as a team – it had all been for the moment when the aliens would make their first move. Now that moment was here: their first ten-thirty – their first red alert.

She glanced across at her commander and saw the look of firm determination on his handsome face. 'It's our first encounter with the new Martians, Tiger,' she began, then paused a second. 'What do you expect?' she asked.

'What do I expect?' Ninestein felt, too, the importance of this initial meeting with Earth's enemies. It might, he reasoned, be the first of many ... or it might be decisive. On this day, the Battle for Earth could be won – or lost. This unseen, unknown aggressor obviously had terrible power and tremendously sophisticated technology. There was something very sinister and threatening about the way they had so easily eluded Lieutenant Hiro and the Spacehawk. It was clear that they were ruthless – the savage destruction of the NASA base on Mars had shown that – and *there* was another instance of the aliens' ability to slip under a radar defence system. Tracking stations on earth had been unable to plot their course, even though their journey from Alpha Centauri had been recorded.

This was a deadly foe – cunning and pitiless. 'What do I expect?' Ninestein pondered. 'I expect … the unexpected.'

As they closed on their objective, Tiger wondered if the location, too, might be an example of the enemy's clever tactics. Below was thick jungle – just the sort of terrain to give the best cover and make things difficult for a search and destroy operation. He decided it was time for the zeroids to play their part. Switching to retro-rockets and down-thrust, he hovered above a small clearing in the under-growth and gave the order for a reconnaissance party to be landed. Three zeroids ejected from the ship and bounced away, out of sight, into the jungle. After a short while, one of them – Zeroid 13 – extended his radio antenna and made an initial report, communicating directly with the sergeant-major.

'Our luck's in,' he said. 'Everything's clear here ... but we'll roll around and check the whole area.' He drew his antenna in. Leading the others, 13 began to roll through the thick undergrowth and tangles of vine. It was part of the genius of zeroid design that their spherical shape allowed maximum propulsion under most conditions. Robots in a humanoid shape encountered the same obstructions as humans might when crossing difficult terrain. A zeroid, instead of having to blast his way through, could simply roll over barriers and hindrances. Their ability to propel themselves through the air meant that chasms and other faults in the earth were no problem – and nor, of course, was hilly or mountainous country as a zeroid would simply roll up one side and down the other. In addition, their shape afforded them better protection than most robots possessed. In times of danger, a visor would close, covering the eyes and other nerve-centres, leaving the zeroid a complete, enclosed ball.

Zero registered the report and began to relay it to Tiger. 'One of my men has just reported—'

'Yeah,' said Ninestein, cutting him off, 'I got it.' As commander, he was plugged in to all communications. To Mary, he said, 'How are we doing?' She was busily monitoring the Battlehawk's systems.

'*We* are doing just fine,' she replied, feeling, perhaps, some of Zero's anxiety for his men. To the sergeant-major, the safety of his troops was all. Mary turned to him. 'If the men we dropped give us a clear, then we'll be landing about ten miles from the energy-source.'

As she spoke, a further report came in from 13. 'Sergeant-major – landing ten-twenty – clear.'

Zero tried again. 'My reconnaissance party …' he began. Ninestein was absorbed in the signals registering on the computer VDU. 'Sir!' Zero's voice was insistent. Ninestein looked up. 'Report that the area *is* safe for landing.'

Ninestein nodded curtly. 'Okay, Mary,' he said, 'take her down.' As Mary set the controls for landing, Tiger gazed ahead, fixedly, deep in thought. Almost to himself, he said, 'A powerful source of energy ... and yet our radar sees nothing.' How could it be, he wondered; how *could* it be? What was out there? Both Mary and Zero registered the concern in his voice. They exchanged a glance. They knew that the commander was fearless – that he would not hesitate to come to grips with any foe. But an enemy you could not see; that emitted a power source that would not register on radar; that could evade the murderous fire power of the mighty Spacehawk – how could you fight such an adversary?

Zeroid 13, together with the other members of the reconnaissance party, stood by as the Battlehawk landed in the clearing. The earsplitting whine of photon-drive in reverse thrust suddenly died, and there was silence. Ninestein turned to the sergeant-major. 'Zero, take your squad to the site of the energy-source and report.'

'Sir!'

'And use reasonable caution. Expect … the unexpected.'

'Yes, Sir.' Zero's antenna shot up. 'Numbers 13, 27 and 35,' he said crisply, 'stand by for patrol.'

From outside came the brisk response: *'Copy! Copy! Copy!'*

'My lucky numbers,' said Zero. 'Well – I'd better get rolling.'

Mary Falconer wondered whether there might not be just a trace of nervousness in Zero's tone. ‘Good luck, Sergeant-major,’ she said.

If it had been possible, a smile of gratitude would have appeared on Zero’s face. ‘Thank you Ma’am.’ He bounced down from his perch and rolled towards the zeroidoor.

‘Take care!’ This time the voice was Ninestein’s, and his meaning was clear – no mistakes!

As Zero disappeared through the zeroidoor, Mary turned to Ninestein. There was a trace of a fond smile on her lips. ‘He’s almost human, isn’t he?’ she remarked.

Ninestein’s response was cool. ‘There’s nothing human about the zeroids, Mary. They’re just machines.’ He went back to examining the VDU for a while, before reflecting: ‘If my theory about that energy-force is correct, I wouldn't send my worst enemy out there.’

‘Out there,’ the sergeant-major was confronting his small patrol. They might have been just machines, but Zero valued their loyalty and unswerving devotion to duty. It was a robot's fate to serve humans – they were programmed for that – and Zero, like his men, would obey any order unhesitatingly. Obedience was the first law of robotics. But was it just a matter of circuits and engineering? The zeroids were the Terrahawks’ infantry: the front-line troops, the scouting parties. The sergeant-major thought of them as brave, resolute fighters. Of course, bravery was a human quality – and robots couldn't possess human feelings, could they? But if that was so, how was it that, as he prepared to lead his patrol into the dense jungle, Sergeant-major Zero felt proud?

'All right, men,' he said brusquely, 'follow me!' Leading the way, he rolled out of sight, 13, 27 and 35 following, towards the unknown.

'Okay, Doctor.' Mary scrutinized the VDU on her control panel. 'I'm taking us to ... Hill 28. That's the best vantage-point.' It was standard action in any Terrahawks battle-plan for Ninestein and Captain Falconer to position themselves on a site overlooking the area of campaign. With satellite back-up from Lieutenant Hiro's Spacehawk, they could then direct operations – and decide best when it was time for them to take part in the action themselves.

With a piercing whine of thrust-motors, the Terrahawk separated itself from the mother-ship. A sleek, angular craft, it looked a little like a precision-built crane-fly. Long legs could be let down from the superstructure so that the craft was able to perch on any surface – and make a getaway in split seconds.

Once they were clear of the Battlehawk, Mary used manual control to fly the short distance to Hill 28. She held the ship on hover for a second or two, while the stilts emerged, then made a perfect landing. Ninestein was showing signs of impatience. 'Come on, Zero,' he muttered. His fingers rapped impatiently on the control panel.

Mary understood something of Tiger's attitude towards the zeroids, and especially his sometimes curt manner towards the sergeant-major. Zero was the last of the prototype zeroids. Unlike the new model, his power nucleus was a unique iranium crystal, quarried on the planet Jupiter. It had very special qualities – qualities that set Zero apart from other zeroids. It made him a natural leader, but it also seemed to provide him with something similar to 'emotions', and that did not fit into Dr Ninestein's theory about what made a good robot. Zero's logic circuits, it appeared, were more subtle – more 'human' – than the Doctor thought they should be.

And yet there was something else behind Tiger's strange relationship with his zeroid sergeant-major. Something Mary thought she could also understand. It was easy to forget the fact, but, of course, Ninestein himself was not human. He was a clone – one of nine. That was how he had got his name: 'Ninestein', for the number of identical models; and 'Tiger', because of the fierce creature which, in common with other cats, was thought to have nine lives. Perhaps, thought Mary, there was something else behind Ninestein's occasional impatience with Zero … something they had in common … a certain longing.

Right now, there was considerable impatience on Ninestein's features. He wanted Zero's report, and he wanted it quickly. Partly to while away the time, and partly to put her theory to the test, Mary asked: 'Tiger, how does it feel to be one of nine clones?'

The commander didn't seem too interested in the question. 'Oh,' he replied casually, 'the same as Zero feels. I mean-he's one of several hundred.'

So, thought Mary, *I could be right.* She risked going a little further. 'You don't like him, do you?'

'Him?' snapped Tiger. '*He* is a robot. I don't think of him as a him; I think of him as an *it*.'

Mary knew that this was the way most people regarded robots. Strangely, she had never quite been able to see them in that light, and especially not the sergeant-major. 'Has it ever occurred to you,' she said, 'that as robots become more advanced, they could develop feelings – like you and me?'

Ninestein's voice softened for a moment. His tone sounded almost humorous. 'Yeah,' he replied, 'it *has* occurred to me.' Then, sounding a great deal more business-like, he flipped a communications switch, and asked: 'Zero, how are we doing?' He couldn't wait any longer for Zero's report.

As if he had anticipated the commander's question, Zero's voice came over the sound-system immediately. Something *was* happening. Ninestein's sixth sense had been working for him again.

'We've located the energy-source, Sir.'

Both Mary and Tiger sat up. 'And what do you see?' queried the Doctor.

In the depths of the jungle, Zero scanned an area directly in front of rum, locking onto the invisible power-source. The radio-pulses were coming directly – and unmistakeably – from beneath the low bough of a fallen tree. Whatever it was lay directly ahead of them, but nothing, absolutely nothing, could be seen.

'The energy-source is under the bough of a tree,' Zero reported. 'I can sense it's there. But I can't see it.'

Ninestein came to a quick decision. 'Zero – fire an energy-bolt at the source. Then beat it!'

There are times when a robot's data-banks receive information that does not seem to compute – and slang is not always properly understood, especially in moments of tension. 'You want me to *beat* it?' Zero gazed in the direction of the invisible enemy and waited for verification of the order.

Mary's voice filtered through the air-waves. ‘Sergeant-major,’ she said, ‘he wants you to ... er ... make a hasty retreat.’

‘*Retreat?*’ There was a mixture of horror and disgust in the zeroid’s voice. Retreat was the last thing he intended. What kind of a zeroid did Ninestein trunk he was? Retreat, indeed!

Tiger had no time for Zero’s ideas of military honour. He yelled an order. ‘Open fire, will you!’ Zero jumped to it. A hatch opened in his casing, to reveal his Energy Bolt Generator, which slid forward and took a bead on the energy-source. Instantly, there was a brilliant flash from the barrel of the EBG and the bough of the tree disintegrated. Zero's circuits computed the result. ‘Doctor!’ His voice was loud with amazement. ‘The energy source is still there, but—’ he reassessed his inbuilt computer reading. ‘But it's moved to one side.’

‘Can you pinpoint it?’ Ninestein wanted to know.

‘No, Sir.’ As a mass of energy, the alien force was registering on Zero's sensors; but he could not find the *object* the energy was coming from.

It's hopeless, thought Ninestein. *The thing is out there –right in front of us– but* ... Suddenly, he had an idea. ‘Use macrovision.’

Zero's eyes came together to form a single viewing unit. Then he rolled forward slightly, so that he was looking at the ground only a few feet away, just in front of the shattered bough. It was as if he were studying an insect in the grass.

Ninestein could hardly contain his impatience. This *had* to work. His fingers rapped away on the console. He was close to exploding with frustration. Mary Falconer decided it was time that she took a hand in things. Gently, she asked, 'What can you see, Sergeant-major?'

An insect! It *was* an insect. And beneath it ... Zero's astonished voice was relayed over the communication channel. 'I see ... I see a space ship ... under a gigantic spider!' Zero stared and stared, bringing the power of his macrovision up to the full. Directly in front of him was what appeared to be a spider the size of a dinosaur. A vast, hairy, evil-looking spider, its eyes flicking menacingly towards Zero, its fangs twitching. And alongside one of its enormous legs, was a space ship, hovering just above the ground. A space ship of a type and design that Zero had never seen before. He realized that the faint humming that he had been able to hear all along, was the ship's power plant.

Zero spoke again, his voice sounding almost panicky. 'It *is* an alien space ship ... and it *is* under a *gigantic spider!*'

That was all Ninestein needed to hear. Using macrovision had been an inspiration. *He* knew, now, what they were up against. 'Okay,' he said to Zero. 'Beat it!' Then, remembering: ‘Er – retreat.’ Mary looked at him, waiting for an explanation.

‘It's an alien space ship, all right,’ he told her, ‘but the spider's not gigantic. The space ship's minute.’

‘Hence no radar echo?’

‘That's right,’ Tiger confirmed.

As he spoke, Mary glanced down at her instrument panel. 'But *we're* getting one now,’ she observed.

In the jungle, Zero reverted to normal vision – and stared in amazement. From the direction of the fallen tree there came a searing flash of white light followed by a deafening, whiplash explosion. The alien ship had grown. No longer was it invisible to the naked eye. It resembled a model of a ship: some two or three feet in length. Then there came another flash, another explosion ... then a series, until the alien craft achieved its full size. It hung, menacingly, some two hundred feet above the jungle floor.

Zero regarded the sinister craft. At last it was out in the open. At last he could see the enemy. ‘Zero to Battlehawk,’ he rapped out. ‘I want fifty men here immediately!’ He had switched to a direct link with the mother-ship.

‘Copy! Copy!’ came the response. The zeroid troops started to roll out of the superstructure. Through the jungle they rolled, at battle-pace, and finalley fell into ranks in front of the sergeant-major.

He wasted no time. ‘Right, you lot.’ His voice bristled with aggression. ‘You know what they say – the bigger they are, the harder they fall. Now – take up your defensive positions.’

From the cockpit of the Terrahawk, high on Hill 28, Mary spotted the action on her VDU. This had not been ordered! Zero was acting on his own initiative! Instead of obeying an order-to retreat- he was *giving* orders. ‘No, Sergeant-major! No!’ she yelled. ‘Return to Battlehawk.’ There was no response. She turned anxiously to Ninestein. ‘He can't hear us!’

The commander’s face was rigid with fury. ‘He doesn't *want* to hear us!’

The zeroids were ready for action; but before Zero could issue a command, a voice was heard, filling the air. A voice from the alien ship. A high-pitched, croaking voice, like that of an aged witch, full of evil. ‘Earthrnan …’ it said.

For a second or two, Zero did not register the full horror of the eerie voice. ‘Earthman’, it had said. ‘Earth*man*’. His pleasure at being called ‘man’ left him off guard. ‘You mean me ... ?’

‘I believe,’ said the unearthly voice, ‘that thirteen is an unlucky number for some people here on earth.' Beside Zero stood the members of the original patrol: 13, 27 and 35. They waited, not knowing what to expect … except the unexpected. When it came, it was with terrible swiftness and force. A sharp *crack* filled the clearing, a shock of white light. 13 exploded like a bomb.

'There … ' said the voice, gloatingly, ' ... I was right.'

It took only a moment for Zero to react. 'Men!' he bellowed. 'Open fire!'

Immediately, the zeroids activated their EBGs and fired bolt after bolt at the enemy. The response from the space-ship was a hail of deadly fire, forcing the zeroids to take evasive action. They redoubled their attack, but to no avail: the alien ship remained undamaged.

From Hill 28, Ninestein called up reinforcements. 'Hawkwing!'

Kate Kestrel heard him and replied. 'Copy.' Her own VDU gave her a picture of the action and of the zeroids' retreat.

'That ship's got a force-field around it,' Tiger informed her. 'We need your help.' Ninestein watched as the energy-bolts discharged by the zeroids bounced off the alien craft's protective shield.

'Hawkwing on ten-forty,' she said. 'Get the zeroids out of there – there's going to be a big bang! Hawkeye – missile mode.'

From the gun-bay came Hawkeye's response. ‘Lock onto target.’

‘Ten-ten,’ Kate confirmed. She banked and began a low, shallow run towards the battle-zone. At the same time, she activated the mechanism which would combine the gun-bay and the control ‘egg’ in which she sat, leaving the wing itself to act as a possible weapon which could home in on any target and ram it, while the ‘egg’ and the gun-bay separated to fly clear at the last minute. Aboard the wing was a massive load of fuel and high explosives.

A hydraulic arm grasped the gun-bay, complete with Hawkeye, and drew it down to lock with the ‘egg’, directly behind Kate's cockpit. She increased power to ‘Max’ and continued her run.

From Terrahawk, Mary watched Kate’s approach. There were only seconds left. ‘Sergeant-major,’ she said, ‘withdraw your men and return to the Battlehawk.’ No response. Mary glanced at Ninestein, anticipating his remark. ‘That's an order!’

Zero heard. But Zero had ideas of his own. ‘If Hawkwing is coming in,’ he said to himself, ‘we must distract the enemy fire.’ He realized that the alien ship could turn its guns on Kate and Hawkeye to devastating effect. ‘Come on, men,’ he urged, 'give them everything you've got.’

As Hawkwing came into view, the zeroids risked everything, coming out of cover and firing ceaselessly at the hovering ship. Ninestein watched Kate's approach on his VDU. 'Don't leave it too late, Kate,' he cautioned.

Kate's eyes were fixed on the target. There had to be perfect, split-second timing, or else … . 'It's never too late, Tiger,' she said. A fraction longer ... just a fraction longer. With a titanic screeching of engines, Hawkwing burst on the scene at max-velocity and rammed the enemy craft. The sky was lit by a series of tearing explosions as the impact blew both ships into a million pieces. From Hill 28, Mary and Tiger saw the blast and for a moment shielded their eyes against the glare. Then they looked again and spotted the 'egg' flying free of the turmoil, its controlling tail fins and fuselage wings swinging out to control its flight.

'Fantastic, Kate! Just fantastic!' Ninestein was jubilant. 'Mind you, in my opinion you left the breakaway dangerously late,' he added.

Despite Tiger's words of caution, Kate was jubilant too. She and Hawkeye had practised that manoeuvre in training a thousand times. But there was nothing like the real thing! Her voice was filled with excitement. 'That had to be the most exciting moment of my life! And I *don't* take chances.' She risked a joke: 'My reflexes are faster than yours – don't forget, I'm younger!'

'True,' replied Ninestein drily, 'but the I'm wiser!'

Another voice came on the air. 'And I'm scared sick,' quipped Hawkeye, 'but then I never was a good passenger.'

The victory celebrations, though, were short-lived. Hearing a blipping sound on the VDU console, Ninestein spun round. He stared at the screen in disbelief 'The energy-force!' he exclaimed. 'It's still there!'

Mary looked at him, shocked. 'But – Kate blew the alien ship apart!' Anxiously, she began to punch buttons on her own console, to see whether the computer could make sense of the impossible. Ninestein's practical brain began to work overtime. 'If they can alter their size,' he reasoned, 'then they must have control over matter ... .'

'The energy-force is still there,' Mary said, scanning the screen in front of her. 'And it's building – *fast!*'

Almost as soon as the words were out of her mouth, both she and Tiger heard a violent crack: the whiplash sound the space ship had made when it changed size. They had a moment to look round, horrified, as the strange craft appeared alongside them, looming up in the Terrahawk's screens like an angel of doom.

Then, at once, there was a second crack. Mary's eyes widened in terror. One minute, the Terrahawks' commander had been next to her. Now he had disappeared. Mary's heart pounded. It couldn't be true ... it *couldn't.* But she continued to stare at the empty space where, a second before, Tiger Ninestein had sat.

The creature looked like a hideous witch from the fairy tales of old. She was grotesquely ugly, her face wizened and twisted, with a hooked nose and yellow, crooked teeth. Her hands were like claws. Her chin was pointed. Vile lumps and warts covered her shrivelled skin. Her hair was a foul, tangled thatch. Ninestein thought he had never seen anyone, or anything, so repulsive.

The interior of the space-ship Ninestein now sat in was bizarre in the extreme. Part of it contained instruments and devices that seemed to be the product of a highly developed technology; but it was furnished as if it had been taken directly from a play about the distant past: the earth, before the Newest Scientific Age. There were hanging curtains, old sofas.... It was as if the aliens had been trying to imitate an earth room and had got the period badly wrong. Ninestein was seated on a plain cube, made of a material he had never encountered before. Some force, strong but invisible, held him motionless.

The crone spoke. It was the same voice that had

echoed in the jungle clearing just before 13 had been destroyed. 'Very stupid, Doctor,' she cackled. 'You should know better than to attack us.' She had said 'us', but, looking round, Ninestein could see no sign of any other alien. The witch-like figure seemed to control the space ship single-handed. *So she knows all about us,* he thought. *She addressed me as 'Doctor'.* Clearly, the aliens' intelligence services were efficient.

He remembered the remains of 13: a tangled wreck of smoking metal in the clearing. 'But *we* did not attack,' he retorted.

'Silence!' The evil creature's voice cracked like a whip. 'How dare you speak to me like that! You – a mere human being!'

Ninestein stared at the humanoid form before him. 'Human ... ' he repeated. 'But aren't you?' To all intents and purposes, hideously ugly though she was, the creature from the planet Guk resembled the life-form called 'human'.

'No!' snapped the alien. 'I am not. My people were once the slaves of humans on our planet. We were their robots.' A note of pride crept into the cracked voice. 'But soon our intellect was greater than that of our creators … so we destroyed them.'

A ghost of Mary Falconer's voice came back to Ninestein: *Has it ever occurred to you that, as robots become more advanced, they could develop feelings?* Feelings for good, she might have added, and feelings for evil. So these creatures had destroyed the human settlers on Guk; had annihilated their masters and had taken over the civilization they had once served. But if they had been robots ... 'You're ... android?' Ninestein queried.

'Yes.' The ugly being drew herself up, as far as her crooked back would allow, in an attempt to look dignified. 'I am Zelda,' she announced, 'and we are androids – in the mould of our creators.'

So that was it, thought Ninestein. They had tried to imitate a human form: and this grotesque thing that stood in front of him was the result. But why should it be so hideous? Then an idea struck him. *In the mould of our creators,* she had said. And they would have chosen to inherit as much knowledge, as much wisdom, from their models as possible, would have wanted, literally, to pick their brains. So, since an android cannot grow like a human … Tiger hazarded a guess.

'A mould based on the oldest and wisest?' he asked.

The witch showed her yellow teeth and preened herself. 'That,' she croaked, 'is why we are so beautiful!' She made a gesture and, from somewhere deep in the ship's hull, came the roar of engines.

From the Terrahawk control, Mary Falconer watched in a daze as the enemy craft lifted off. She had no idea what to do – or where Tiger had gone.

His sudden disappearance, though, had registered on the sensor-probes of the rest of the Hawkwing team. Anxiously, they called for information.

'Central Control,' the voice was that of Kate Kestrel, 'are you receiving me? Mary – are you all right?'

'This is Sergeant-major Zero calling for a copy! Doctor! What is your ten-twenty?'

There was no reply. Zero's computer circuits whirred, trying to formulate a solution to the mystery. The zeroid's eyes whizzed round in confusion. 'The whole thing,' he said agitatedly, 'is beyond my comprehension.'

On the flight deck of her ship, Zelda screeched with laughter over their confusion. Then she turned back to the Doctor. 'On our flight to Mars,' she reminded him, 'we will have to pass your gunship?'

'Spacehawk? It will blast us out of the sky,' Ninestein assured her. 'And my theory is that you have insufficient power left to reduce your ship's size – or to maintain its force-field.' He realized that Zelda must have used enormous reserves of energy during the battle; and even more in the process of matter-control that had enabled her to slip past Hiro on her way to Earth and appear as nothing more than an energy-source until the time had come to switch back to full size.

The android laughed. ‘Correct,’ she said. ‘But they won't fire with you aboard.’

‘They don’t know I’m aboard.’

‘They will – because you are going to tell them. Just speak – and they will hear.’

The space ship, Ninestein realized, was patched-in to all Terrahawks’ sound systems. ‘Hiro,’ he said, ‘can you hear me?’

The lieutenant's voice rang out in the cabin. ‘I hear you, Doctor.’ There was a moment's pause; then he went on: ‘Where *are* you?’

‘I’m aboard the Martian ship. It has insufficient power to maintain its force-field. If you open fire you will destroy it.’ Zelda watched him, grinning evilly. Then the grin was wiped from her face, as she heard Tiger say: ‘So – open fire! That’s an order, Hiro!’

Zelda boggled for an instant. Then she laughed even louder. ‘He won’t fire – not with you aboard. You’re corning with me to Mars. And then we’ll take you apart to see what makes you tick.’

Just as they did with their human masters, thought Tiger. But there was something that Zelda did not know. Tiger smiled grimly.

'You've slipped up, android. I'm only one of nine clones. Kill me and there will be another Ninestein within twenty-four hours.'

For the first time, Zelda's hideous face showed signs of panic. *A clone!* She knew well enough what that meant. The replacement commander would not just look like Ninestein, he would *be* Ninestein - with all Ninestein's knowledge, skill, determination ... and courage.

Hiro had not been the only one to hear Tiger's order. Kate and Hawkeye had picked up the transmission and had immediately plotted a course that would enable them to track the alien ship as it thundered towards outer space. From the cockpit of the 'egg', Kate looked out at the retreating craft with Tiger and Zelda aboard. 'What do we do, Hawkeye?' She sounded desperate.

'There's not much we can do, Kate, except tail it.'

Kate consulted her instrument panel. They were dangerously high. 'But we're already on the fringe of space,' she told him despairingly.

'Then it's all up to Hiro.'

Up to Hiro? His only move – the only positive thing he *could* do – was obey orders; and that would mean blasting Zelda's ship. And Zelda. And Commander Ninestein. 'But he can't … ' began Kate; she left the rest of the sentence unsaid, and addressed her next remark directly to the Japanese lieutenant over the ship-to-ship airwave. 'Don't do it, Hiro! Please don't destroy that ship!' There was no answer. Kate's voice became shrill. 'Hiro! Do you copy?'

He could hear her. But he knew that the decision was his alone. Ninestein had given him a direct order. And Hiro was not the kind of officer who disobeyed a direct order. He must carry out the instruction. He must turn the Spacehawk's deadly guns on Zelda's craft. And on Tiger. He must give the order to fire. And yet … .

101 was connected to the computer console, ready to relay the order to the gunners. Hiro turned to the space sergeant. 'What would you do, 101?' The zeroid answered at once: 'It's not for us to make decisions.'

True enough, thought Hiro; they were programmed to obey. Even so, who else could he turn to? And he knew that the zeroids – some of them – could bypass certain circuits and think for themselves. 'But you can,' he said, 'if you want to.'

101 knew that there were only seconds left before a decision must be made. He knew what was at stake. And he knew that this had to be a

human decision. 'The Doctor,' he said, 'would not like *us* to start making decisions.'

Hiro sighed. Of course, the zeroid was correct. Ninestein did not hold with zeroids that thought rather than obeyed. Hiro was the officer in charge. Hiro must give the order. 'You're right,' he said. '*I* must make the decision.' He looked at the tracking coordinates on his VDU. The enemy ship was in range now. Shortly, it would be past them, free, on its way to Mars with no-one and nothing to stop it.

'101 ,' he said. But the order would not pass his lips; the words seemed to stick in his throat. '101—' The space sergeant waited, poised to pass on the instruction. The lieutenant's whole body trembled with tension.

'101!' Still Hiro hesitated. Then: '101! Open fire!' The space sergeant relayed the message to the porthole gunners. Immediately, they released a shattering broadside.

'Oh, my God!' wailed Hiro. What had he done? He watched as the terrifying power of the zeroid EBGs smashed into the alien ship, destroying it completely. A million pieces of wreckage exploded into space. *The commander,* he thought, *I've killed Dr Ninestein!*

His thoughts were echoed by Mary Falconer as she sat in the Terrahawk, unable to take in the horror of what had just happened. But before she could speak or react in any way, there came a whip-lash crack. Mary leapt with shock. Tiger Ninestein sat next to her.

Finally, Mary managed to find her voice. 'Tiger!' she exclaimed. 'Thank God you're all right!'

Ninestein looked calm and controlled. He flicked a switch on his VDU to bring up the lieutenant's image. 'Well done, Hiro,' he said.

Hiro's shock was as great as Mary's. All he could manage to say was: 'What on earth are you doing there?'

Ninestein smiled. 'You mean what am I doing here on Earth,' he quipped. He imagined the rest of the Terrahawk crew listening in, and decided he had better explain. It must have seemed, after all, as if he were signing his own death warrant when he had ordered Hiro to fire. 'Well, I had this theory – and it's relatively complicated, but I figured that if their ship was destroyed, their power to hold me would also be destroyed.'

Fine as a theory , thought Mary, *but supposing* ... . All she said was: 'And you were right.'

Ninestein smiled grimly. 'I'm glad to say.' It had been a risk – a terrible risk; but, so far, his theories about the aliens had been correct. Over the radio-link, he issued an order to the sergeant-major.

'Zero, we are rejoining Battlehawk. I want you back on board.'

Zero, like the others, was more than a little relieved to hear the commander's voice. But there was something he had to do before returning to the mother-ship. 'Yes, Sir,' he replied. 'If you could just give me a few minutes... .'

Anger mounted in Tiger. That confounded zeroid – thinking for himself again. He had already disobeyed one direct order that day when Mary had instructed him to leave the battle-zone as Hawkwing approached. Now here he was again, questioning a command instead of leaping to it, as a robot should. Tiger opened his mouth to yell; but Mary, sensing what the sergeant-major might mean, cut in.

'That's all right, Sergeant-major,' she said; and then, to pacify Tiger, she added: 'It'll be a few minutes before we get back ourselves.' She glanced over at Ninestein, silently pleading with him. Tiger stayed silent.

Sergeant-major Zero stood in the clearing, accompanied by three of his troops. Nearby was a small, circular mound of earth. Scraped on the surface of the mound was the number 13. Other zeroids stood a little way back, awaiting instructions. Zero was quiet for a moment. Then he gave the order: 'Present *arms.'* Each zeroid extended his EBG. 'Fire!' roared Zero. A volley of energy bolts were loosed into the sky. There was another moment of silence; then the guard of honour retracted weapons.

'Sergeant-major – ' It was the voice of zeroid 35.

'Sergeant-major, I don't understand. I mean ... when we get back, they'll make another number 13, won't they?'

Of course they would, thought Zero, of course they would. But that wasn't the point. Here was a zeroid – one of his *men* – who had fallen in battle. Yes, of course they could make another 13. But ... .

Turning to 35, he said, with great feeling, 'You know your trouble, 35: you've got no heart!'

'Zero!' Ninestein's patience had finally run out.

'Sir!' Zero leaped as if he had been stung. 'Right men,' he urged, 'let's get rolling. At the double!' Within minutes, the zeroid army was back aboard the Battlehawk, and lifting off, as Mary and Doctor Ninestein, from the Terrahawk flight-deck atop the mother-ship, raised the photon-drive towards full power.

Chapter Three

The alien space ships came roaring in, holding a tight formation. Tiger Ninestein held his fire until the critical moment, then unleashed a barrage of shots, bringing four of them down in quick succession. His pulse raced. The score on the VDU screen read 738. He was going to beat that record of 749! He waited for the next attack.

Sergeant-major Zero entered through the zeroidoor and bounced up onto his perch in the Terrahawk. 'You wanted to see me.' Zero glanced over Ninestein's shoulder at the score. Tiger ignored him … or had not .heard him. *'Sir!'* Zero insisted. After all, like a good zeroid, he had come in response to a direct order from the commander.

Hearing Zero's raised voice, Tiger looked up. As he did so, an invader destroyed his video-ship. He looked down in horror. The score was wiped out and the screen went dead. He threw the game-control onto the console in front of him and strode over to confront Zero.

'Yes Sergeant-major,' he said icily, 'I wanted to see you. Today you disobeyed an order. You started to think for yourself. Well, I've got news for you. *You* are a machine. *You* are nothing. *You* are – *zero.* You are absolute *zero.* Get it?'

If robots could flinch, Zero would have done.

'Doctor–' he began. But Ninestein was not inclined to listen.

'Don't "Doctor" me,' he retorted angrily. 'In future, if I say jump, you *jump!*' This time he did pause for a response. There was silence. 'Well,' he insisted, 'don't just sit there. Say something.'

Zero's sensors had picked up another presence in the room. To cover his confusion, he said: 'Yes, Doctor ... ah – there's someone here to see you.'

Kate and Mary had come into the room while Tiger had been yelling at Zero. He had been so preoccupied with giving the sergeant-major a dressing-down, that he had not noticed them. 'Why girls,' he said, 'I didn't know you were there.' He sounded more than a trifle embarrassed.

Both of the women looked at him disapprovingly, Mary in particular. 'Obviously!' she retorted. Then she advanced to face him. 'I happen to think that Sergeant-major Zero behaved like a real man today.'

Before Ninestein could recover himself, Kate joined in. 'That's right! And if he hadn't drawn the enemy fire, Hawkeye and I might not have been here tonight for the party.'

'Party?' It was the first Ninestein had heard of a party. The girls' expressions softened. 'Yes,' said Kate, taking his arm and drawing him towards the door. 'In the White House. Come on.'

The three of them left. At first, there was silence in the Terrahawk. Then the sergeant-major hopped off his perch and bounced round the control-room in an ecstatic burst of joy. 'I happen to think,' he crowed, bouncing gleefully, 'Sergeant-major Zero behaved,' his bounces grew higher and more erratic, 'like a real man today.' From ceiling to floor, he went, in a frenzy of happiness. 'A real man,' he repeated, over and over. 'A *m-a-n!'*

The party went with a swing – or, in the case of Zero, who had been invited to join it – with a bounce. Kate was entertaining her fellow Terrahawks with one of her own compositions, when Ninestein raised a hand for silence. The time had come, he decided, for a few words of congratulation.

'Okay, folks,' he said, as the others fell silent, 'let's raise our glasses. Today, we had our first encounter with the "New Martians" –' he paused for effect, '– and we won! C-I-G.' And when his officers looked a little puzzled at hearing this apparently new coded instruction, he explained: 'Champagne Is Go!'

Nearby, Zero uttered a tiny *hic.* From his perch behind the Doctor, he had snaked out a tube from one of the tiny hatches in his casing and stealthily drained Tiger's glass. 'Actually, Sir ... it's Champagne Is Gone!' Even Ninestein joined in the laughter. Then he continued: 'If only Hiro were here with us tonight.' He reflected on the crucial and courageous role the Japanese lieutenant had played - obeying orders, as he had been taught, and destroying Zelda's ship so that Ninestein could be released from its power. 'But,' he reminded them, 'someone has to remain on watch.'

It was almost as if, by speaking Hiro's name, Tiger had summoned him up. Over the White House tannoy, Hiro's voice could be heard, calling urgently. 'Doctor! Dr Ninestein!'

Tiger looked round in surprise. For a moment, he almost believed that Hiro *had* joined the party. Then he took out his pocket-communicator, and pressed the 'open' button. 'Yes, Hiro?'

In Spacehawk, orbiting high above the Earth, Hiro looked to 101 for confirmation of the information he had just been given. The zeroid was plugged into the central computer and relaying its findings. The computer was never wrong. There could be no mistake. When he spoke, the lieutenant's voice was filled with alarm. 'Zelda!' The name resounded in the now utterly still room at the White House. 'She's on her way back!'

Ninestein's eyes widened in disbelief. 'But that's impossible,' he said.

The words were scarcely out of his mouth, when another - terrifying and familiar - voice filled the White House; the Terrahawks crew listened in horror as Zelda's words came to them over their own tannoy system.

'Nothing in this universe of ours is impossible. You should have known that, Doctor! When my ship lost its power to control matter, you were automatically returned to Earth-and *I* to Mars.'

So that was it, thought Ninestein. His theory had been correct, all right, but it had saved Zelda as well as himself. The evil witch had not been destroyed in the space-shattering explosion. She was alive, and well, and returning to Earth. The party was over – in more ways than one. Members of the Terrahawks unit stood spellbound, their glasses of champagne forgotten now, and their victory celebrations a cruel joke, waiting to hear what their enemy would say next.

'But fear not,' the hag's voice continued, 'for despite your hostility, I return to Earth – in peace.'

'Peace?' echoed Ninestein. He paused only for a second before rapping out the order: 'Battle stations!'

Kate and Hawkeye left, at the double, to put Hawkwing on standby; Zero sped back to the Terrahawk; Ninestein wasted no time in using the outer-space eyes of the Spacehawk to keep trace of Zelda's progress. 'Give me an update, Hiro,' he ordered.

'She's coming into firing range,' the lieutenant told him. 'What are your orders, Doctor?'

Ninestein was in no doubt. 'Whatever she says,' he cautioned, 'we know she's hostile. If she gets any closer – let her have it!'

'Ten-ten,' responded Hiro.

Zelda's ability to listen in to the Terrahawks' radio wavelength had enabled her to speak directly to Ninestein a moment before; now it gave her advance warning of the Doctor's intentions. Before her ship came within range of the Spacehawk's gun, she activated the photonic retros in her craft's hull; there was a brief blaze of light, and the alien ship slowed; then, finally, it came to a full stop.

101, still connected to the computer, detected the change in velocity. 'Alien ship has fired retros,' he told Hiro, 'and is now stationary.'

'Thank you 101.' Hiro relayed the information back to Earth. 'Doctor! Zelda's ship is standing off, just out of range.'

'All right, Hiro. We're on a ten-forty down here. I'm going to the Terrahawk. Keep your eyes peeled. And –'

Hiro knew what was coming next. Silently, he mouthed the words as Ninestein spoke them.

'–expect the unexpected.'

Hiro grinned. All he said was: 'Ten-ten.' Despite his smile, though, he was apprehensive. He had already seen something of Zelda's awesome powers. He glanced at 101. The zeroid was busily monitoring impulses from the computer. Robot and human alike were waiting for the next move- and knew it would have to come from the enemy. The atmosphere on the Spacehawk's flight-deck was tense.

The lieutenant jumped as Zelda's voice suddenly echoed round his ship.

'Earthmen ... ' The cracked tones were coaxing, almost treacly. 'Earthmen, I come on a goodwill mission. I bring a gift from my people. I request safe conduct to your base so that I may confer with your commander.'

Hiro would have none of it. 'Our base is concealed,' he told her. 'It's position is revealed to no-one.

'Of course!' Zelda did her best to sound hurt. 'Because we are alien to you, you automatically assume us to be hostile.'

Hiro felt a tiny prick of conscience. He knew that the Inter-universe Code demanded that all visitors from other planets, all aliens, should be treated with respect unless they showed clear signs of aggression. But Zelda *had* been aggressive – hadn't she? Until the moment of 13's destruction in the jungle clearing, Hiro would have been prepared to give Zelda the benefit of the doubt. No-one knew exactly what had happened when the aliens had reached Mars. Perhaps someone on the NASA station had panicked and fired first. Who could be sure that these were the *same* aliens who had first attacked Earth in a lightning raid years ago, when the UN High Command had first asked Ninestein to form Terrahawks? Well, Ninestein seemed sure; and there was the evidence of the wanton destruction of Zeroid 13.

'No,' Hiro replied, anxious to show that he respected Inter-universe law, 'no, *I* didn't think that. I was prepared to believe you were friendly, but then you attacked us.'

Zelda was ready for this. '*I* didn't attack. I defended myself. One of *your* robots attacked *me*.'

'That's impossible,' retorted Hiro. 'They weren't ordered to attack.'

'But they can think for themselves – can they not?' It was Zelda's trump card. Overhearing it, 101 nodded. No-one liked to admit it, but ... .

'No they can't,' Hiro asserted. Then his voice became less certain. 'Well ... they shouldn't ... .'

From the Hawknest, Ninestein was listening to this exchange. Now he turned to Sergeant-major Zero, his face grim. 'Well?' he asked.

Zero contrived to look outraged. His eyes rotated. 'I can assure you, Sir, that Number 13 did not fire first.'

Ninestein looked at him, levelly. He was remembering the zeroid's convenient deafness when an order had been given to retreat. 'But you have been "thinking" lately – right?'

Zero did not see the importance of the question immediately. 'Thinking', just like a human, like a 'man'; deciding to act on his own initiative … Oh, yes, he'd been doing some of that, all right. He, and some of the others, weren't just the slavish machines that everyone took them for.

'Oh, yes, Sir,' he answered proudly.

Tiger gave him a hard look. Then he swivelled his chair in order to face the control console, and locked the communications channel on to a new frequency. Speaking to the lieutenant, he said: 'Stay on this multi-frequency channel, Hiro – we don't want Zelda to overhear us.' He threw another sharp glance in the direction of the sergeant-major, before continuing. 'Zero has been "thinking" again, so it's possible – just possible – that she's right. Maybe Number 13 *did* shoot first.' The unspoken thought hung in the air: maybe the zeroid commander had decided to give an order without first having received one.

Zero's voice was filled with outrage. 'I have never, *never* disobeyed an order!'

'Oh, *sure* ...' Ninestein replied.

Aboard Hawkwing, Kate and Hawkeye listened as the commander gave them instructions to patrol and keep observation during Zelda's descent.

Zelda's descent! Hawkeye, for one, could not believe it. 'You know something, Kate?' he paused for effect. 'Tiger's crazy.'

Kate was pretty puzzled by their commander's actions, too. Had not Tiger been the one who had warned them of the aliens' hostility during their training programme. He had always seemed sure of it. Now it looked as if he were going soft. She searched for a reason.

'I guess he wants to give that creature the benefit of the doubt.' Hawkeye was not likely to feel the same way. He said: 'Yeah, some of my best friends are androids,' but he made the word 'androids' sound a lot like 'rattlesnakes'.

Ninestein's voice broke in on their conversation. 'Hawkwing, you have a ten-fifty.'

‚Ten-ten,' replied Kate. To Hawkeye, she said: 'Here we go!'

Projected by its giant catapult, the Hawkwing took just ten seconds to reach launch velocity of 750 feet per second from a standing start. The waters of the lake revolved and formed their vortex. The ship tore along the solid tunnel of water and out into the hot, blue South American sky.

In the Terrahawk, Zero sat on his perch and sulked. He had closed the eye-shutters in his casing. Ninestein ignored him.

On the multi-frequency channel he had used to communicate with Hiro, he said, 'Kate, Hawkeye, you know the drill. Circle the landing area. If Zelda makes one hostile move- blast her!'

'Ten-ten.' That's a bit more like it, thought Hawkeye. Even so, he was still worried by the notion of actually letting Zelda land.

Mary Falconer felt the same. She recalled what had happened when the aliens had first touched down on Earth, a few brief hours ago. She recalled, too, the panic she had felt when she had realized that Ninestein had vanished from the seat next to hers, to be transported to the enemy ship by means of some kind of evil magic. She glanced anxiously at Tiger, but tried to keep her tone of voice light. 'Same time, same place, huh? Don't you think she's deceiving you?'

Tiger's response was to turn to Zero. The sergeant-major's eyes were partially uncovered; on catching Tiger's glance, he slammed them shut again.

'Well,' said the commander meaningfully, '*someone's* deceiving me.' He prepared the controls for lift-off.

Mary remained uncertain. 'Tiger,' she asked, 'don't you think we should take a battalion of zeroids with us?'

'I'm not using zeroids again until we know the truth. If we get into trouble, we know that Hawkwing can zap that ship – and, anyway we've got the Battlehawk.' The controls, now, were all 'Go'.

'Hold tight Sergeant-major,' Mary cautioned. 'We're going to ten-fifty.'

There was no response. Zero remained immobile.

'Didn't you hear what the lady said?' asked Ninestein. Still no response. He shrugged. 'Suit yourself.' The pitch of the engines rose and the Battlehawk's nose swung up to the vertical. Ninestein activated full-thrust. The White House opened like a flower as the great ship rose. At the last minute, unseen by either of the pilots, Zero's stabilizers shot out and locked in to take-off position.

'Tiger,' Mary said, levelling the Battlehawk's flight once they were clear, 'what do you think Zelda really has in store for us?'

Ninestein detected the uncertainty in her voice, but all he said was: 'Well, as I always say … (Mary knew what was coming) '... expect the unexpected.' As he spoke the last word, he whipped round in his chair and caught the sergeant-major with eyes wide open, watching every move, and, quite clearly, listening to every word. A fraction late, the zeroid snapped *his* visor shut and pretended to be un-interested in the proceedings. Tiger almost permitted himself a smile.

Aboard the Hawkwing, Kate Kestrel was echoing Mary's worried question. 'Hawkeye,' she asked the gunnery officer, 'what goodies do you think Zelda's got for us?' She was referring to the 'gift' that the wizened android had promised.

Hawkeye chuckled. 'I don't know, Kate, but,' and he tapped the firing-lever on his control panel, 'I certainly know what I've got for her if there's any trouble.'

Like Kate's, though, his curiosity was aroused. Using the ship-to-ship channel, he asked Hiro the same question. 'What do *you* think our friend from Mars is going to bring? War – or peace?'

Hiro was still confused. He simply did not know what to think. On the one hand, there had been that vicious shoot-out and the end of Number 13; on the other, Zelda had sounded so sincere. 'Well, Hawkeye – er – well – I've always firmly believed it is wrong to assume aliens hostile simply because they're alien—'

There was something in his voice that made Hawkeye uneasy. 'But—' he put in.

'But,' Hiro continued, 'I don't believe our zeroids could lie.' Standing next to him, Space Sergeant 101 offered a silent comment. He nodded – *oh yes they could.*

Hiro went on: 'I mean, they were never programmed to lie.' I01 shook his head this time, agreeing. *No, they were never programmed to do that; however ... .*

Listening to Hiro, Hawkeye put two and two together – and came up with something a lot like four. 'You don't trust her.'

'No,' said Hiro, a little reluctantly, 'I don't.'

As the ship continued its descent to Earth, Zelda listened to this conversation. Unlike the multi-frequency channel, the ship-to-ship was not secure.

She grinned, baring the hideous, deformed, yellow teeth. Then her gargoyle's face twisted as the grin became a laugh.

'We know what's in store for our little Earthlings, don't we?' she cackled. 'We are going to give them lots of little presents, aren't we?' She appeared to be addressing her remarks to a stack of mysterious looking cubes, talking to them as if they were children.

Her horrible laugh grew louder as she thought about her plan – the plan that would mean the end for Ninestein. The more she thought of it, the louder she laughed, throwing back her misshapen head and tugging gleefully at the dry, stringy hanks of hair that sprouted from her head, until the whole ship rang with her cracked, hysterical mirth.

Same time, same place, Mary Falconer had said. Tiger might have his doubts about who had fired first, she thought, but he was not going so far as to let Zelda anywhere near the White House, as she had requested. The coordinates he had given the android would bring her down on the same spot as before. She wondered if Tiger's idea was to make Zelda believe that the Terrahawk base lay somewhere nearby.

They homed in on the jungle clearing and touched down. Immediately, doors in the belly of the Battlehawk swung open and a second roar of engines overlaid the Battlehawk's reverse-thrust motors. Slowly, descending by means of its multi-directional jet thrusts, a large vehicle, with tracks instead of wheels, came into view. It made the short trip from the mother-ship's fuselage, grounded, and then drove clear.

The Battletank was one of the Unit's 'surprise' weapons. Its purpose was conventional ground attack: getting to places on the earth's surface where the airborne craft could not go. And, just as it could be dropped from the Battlehawk's fuselage, so it could be scooped up by the big ship in flight, and carried to a safe refuge if need be. It was manned by two megazoids, zeroid-types which were much bigger, but less complex than the regular robot force.

It was to these two 'men' that Ninestein spoke, as soon as the Battletank had taken up its position some distance from the main ship.

'Megazoids: guard the Battlehawk, okay?' Hearing their 'Ten-ten', Tiger left the control panel in the Terrahawk and made for a door at the side of the cockpit. As he passed Zero's perch, he could not resist saying, 'Let's hope we can trust your big brothers.'

The sergeant-major kept a dignified silence, watching Ninestein as he disappeared through the door. After a second or two, a faint electronic hum filled the central control area. Zero rotated on his perch to face Mary. 'He's committing all his knowledge to the computer data dump?' he queried.

Zero had a reason for asking; he had been doing a lot of serious 'thinking' during the flight.

Mary confirmed the fact. It was standard practice for officers of Ninestein's particular type. 'Yes, Sergeant-major. If anything should happen to him– ' she paused. 'Heaven forbid!

But if it did, then one of his eight clones would take over.'

'And pick up all his – er – knowledge, as it were?' Zero wanted to know.

'From the data dump,' Mary nodded. 'That's right.'

'So if anything … happened to him––' Zero hesitated, wondering if he might be going too far; then he decided to risk it: '–like he ceased to function.'

Mary did not beat about the bush. 'You mean, if he were killed in action?'

'Well, yes ... .' Zero gazed moodily at the door of the data dump and spoke what was in his 'mind'. 'Then his replacement clone would *still* mistrust me,' he said gloomily.

Mary saw where he had been leading. 'I'm afraid so, Sergeant-major.' Once more, Zero's eye-visor slammed shut.

Leaving the data dump, his complete up-to-date knowledge securely stored in its circuits, Ninestein returned to his console and tuned-in to Lieutenant Hawkeye's tannoy. 'Hawkwing,' he said, 'what's Zelda's ten-twenty?'

High above the scene, Hawkeye took readings on the approaching craft. 'She's about thirty miles south. She'll be landing in a few minutes.'

'Ten-ten.'

Kate Kestrel decided it was time to put Hawkwing's standard practice into operation.

‘We’re going to a full ten-forty, Tiger,’ she advised. Then, to Hawkeye, she said: ‘Shotgun – do you feel like a piggy-back?’

'Stand by to receive boarders,' came the response.

The hydraulic arm hissed out and lowered the gun-bay onto the ‘egg’. As soon as she was sure it was secure, Kate let Ninestein know.

‘Hawkwing at ten-forty.’

‘Ten-ten.’

‘Here she comes!’ – this was Mary. Tiger looked up to see Zelda’s ship settle in the clearing, some distance from the Battlehawk. Her engines wound down. Finally, they stopped. No sound could be heard apart from the continual prattle of insects. Both sides waited. In the Terrahawk, Mary Falconer felt her heartbeat grow faster.

It was Zelda who broke the silence. On the tannoy, her voice was loud and shrill. ‘Well, Doctor, you gave me safe passage to Earth. Do I take it that I have your confidence?’

Ninestein’s answer was cool. ‘You have not won our confidence,’ he warned her. ‘Not yet; but, for the moment, we are prepared to give you the benefit of the doubt.’ Behind him, Zero revolved his eyes in exasperation.

‘Very wise, Doctor, you are very wise.’ Was there something sinister in Zelda’s tone: a hint of laughter, perhaps? She went on: ‘As you know, I have the power to control matter. I will now perform a small miracle for you. Look to the west, Doctor – the land is bright.'

This is it, thought Ninestein. *Whatever she's got planned - this is it.* He gestured towards the radio, fixed on the multi-frequency channel. Mary lowered her voice to a whisper, knowing that Zelda was tuned to the Battlehawk's control centre so that she and Ninestein could communicate.

'Kate – Hawkeye—' Mary put her lips close to the transmitter. 'Stand by!'

'Ten-ten,' came Kate Kestrel's hushed reply.

Tiger kept his eyes fixed on the western horizon – or as much of it as the jungle would allow him to see. As he watched, a low hum began, gathering pitch and strength. It seemed to be coming from Zelda's ship. The power, and the noise, grew until it was almost unbearable. Then, with no warning, a scanner-device appeared on the dome of the alien space ship.

'What is she doing?' Mary's voice was filled with anxiety.

Sergeant-major Zero decided to abandon his sulk. 'Don't trust her, Sir,' he pleaded.

Zelda's ship began to give off flashes of light, bathing the trees around the clearing in an orange-white glow. Still the noise grew, battering the eardrums of the watchers. Then there came a heart- stopping explosion, a tremendous clap of thunder accompanied by an almost blinding streak of light, like a thunderbolt. The lightning appeared to strike the ground about a hundred feet ahead of the Battlehawk. Over the tannoy came the wild, crazed shrieking of Zelda's laughter.

Mary turned to Ninestein in alarm. 'Tiger- she'll kill us all.' Ninestein was inclined to think the same.

Speaking into the radio, he said: 'Hawkwing - ram that ship!'

'Ten-ten,' yelled Kate. *Thank Heaven for that*, she thought. It was a little difficult to tell what was going on down there, but with Zelda's thunder and lightning roaring around the place, it did not seem the time to pull any punches. She banked the Hawkwing and put it into a steep dive.

Below, there was a searing wave of light and a whiplash *crack* so loud that a thunderbolt seemed to have landed directly in the clearing. Watching, Mary thought, for a moment, that the Hawkwing had made its strike. Then, as the brilliance faded, she could see – and Ninestein could see – what had happened. Zelda had delivered her gift. Stretching away into the distance was a road, where before there had been only thick jungle. A magnificent highway, running like a ribbon over hill and valley, to the far horizon. A miracle, indeed.

Tiger was transfixed for a moment. Then, grabbing the console microphone, he yelled, 'Hawkwing! Pull out!'

No-one else could have done it. The Hawkwing was less than a second away from its crash-course objective. But no-one else had Kate Kestrel's reactions. Without having to think, she moved her hand from the control that would have released the 'egg', taking herself and Hawkeye to safety, switched the wing off automatic, and brought her craft round in a screaming arc, missing the alien ship by inches. It was only after the manoeuvre was complete that she bothered to acknowledge the order. 'Ten-ten,' she said coolly.

From the gun-bay Hawkeye looked down at the shining road: a black river, carved through the jungle and unwinding as far as the eye could see.

'It *is* a miracle,' he said in awe. 'It's magnificent!'

Ninestein, looking out from the Terrahawk agreed. Zelda's ability to control matter was a gift that could be used for evil – or for good. To be able to plough a superb road like this through a wild jungle – and all in a matter of seconds – would certainly be a blessing to mankind. The possibilities, the *peaceful* possibilities, of matter-control were endless.

As if she were reading his mind, Zelda spoke again. ‘You have received your first gift. Just imagine what other benefits I could bring to your planet. Now I will leave. I take it that I have safe conduct?’

Tiger continued to gaze at the road. He seemed to be deep in thought. ‘Yes ... Yes, Zelda. You have my word.’ Then, to make sure of the fact, he spoke to Hiro. ‘Lieutenant, did you get that?’

‘Yes, I got that, Doctor. We'll stay well out of range.’ Nonetheless, there was uncertainty in his voice. 101 was not convinced, either.

‘Sir,’ ventured the robot, ‘I know Sergeant-major Zero like – er –’ He searched for a human phrase that would express what he meant, ‘– like he was my brother. And I know he would not have attacked that alien ship without a good reason.’

Hiro’s loyalty to Commander Ninestein was absolute. Even so, he did not trust Zelda – and he *did* trust 101 and the zeroid force. ‘Exactly,’ he muttered.

As the alien ship wound its motors up for take-off, Mary Falconer turned to the commander. ‘You're going to let her go?’

Ninestein’s tone was firm. ‘I believe there’s been ... a misunderstanding.’

Zero’s eyes lowered in shame. Surely Tiger couldn’t really believe that he ... .

Mary looked worried. 'Are you *sure,* Tiger?'

He did not reply. Instead, he turned to the console-mike and said: 'Zelda, you're clear to leave.'

'Thank you, Commander.'

Zero bounced down from his perch and crossed to the control area to watch the murderess – the killer of his trooper Number 13 – getting away scot-free. Over the roar of photon-drive engines, they could hear Zelda's mad, cackling laughter. The gift – the road – lay before them. But there were other 'gifts', something they did not know about, that the cunning android had left behind.

'The Road to Mandalay,' murmured Tiger, thoughtfully.

'Road to Mandalay?' Mary was puzzled.

'It's an old song.'

'Sung by grandfather?' she asked lightly.

Tiger's reply had a touch of bitterness about it. 'I didn't have a grandfather,' he reminded her. 'I had a test tube. I'm a clone – remember?'

Mary could have bitten her tongue off. 'Tiger,' she stammered, 'I ... I'm so sorry. I didn't mean to ... .'

Ninestein knew that she had spoken without thinking. Mary would be the last person to say something deliberately hurtful. To save her embarrassment, he said: 'Mary, why don't we take my old Roller and get a look at that highway.'

Zero's eyes bulged. *Old Roller!* What a way to describe the zeroid-in-chief.

Tiger caught his look. 'Not you, Zero,' he said patiently. 'My Roller ....' Zero looked blank. 'My Rolls-Royce,' the commander explained.

Zero remembered – in fact, if he were to tell the truth, he had known all along what Ninestein meant. He just did not like to admit that the commander possessed other machines that he thought highly of … perhaps even preferred!

Mary, on the other hand, was completely in the dark. *Roller,* she thought. *A Rolls-Royce?* In the Twenty-first Century, when inter-planetary travel was as common as riding on an aeroplane had once been; when the earth could be circumnavigated in a matter of minutes? Still, she reflected, with Ninestein, anything was possible. As the commander himself might say: you had to expect the unexpected.

Tiger operated a few levers on the control panel, then led the way out of the ship and into the clearing. Together, he and Mary stood by the newly created road. A ramp had lowered at the front of the Battlehawk. With a slightly impish grin, Ninestein put two fingers into his mouth and gave off a shrill, two-tone whistle. At once, the unmistakeable radiator-grille of a Rolls-Royce appeared and the car glided down the ramp and onto the road. Mary's astonishment was complete when she realized that the beautiful car had no driver.

She gazed in astonishment for a second or two, before saying, 'You didn't tell me … .'

Tiger smiled mysteriously. 'Well, I don't tell you everything.'

He gestured proudly towards the car. 'Thirty-five years old,' he boasted, 'and just like the day she– ' he corrected himself, '–I mean *he,* was born.'

Mary did not notice the change of gender. 'She's beautiful.'

'Yep,' Tiger agreed. 'Totally restored.' But there was more to this particular Rolls-Royce than met the eye. 'A few alterations,' he said. 'A new power-plant, new interior, all the latest technology.' Then almost as an afterthought, he said: 'And it can think – and speak – for itself.' The commander's face glowed with pride.

'Like Zero,' Mary remarked, teasingly.

Ninestein looked faintly shocked. '*Not* like Zero! *This* machine has breeding.'

It was just as well, Mary thought, that the sergeant-major was still in the Terrahawk. It would have taken him a long time to get over that last remark.

The car purred up to where they stood and came to a smooth halt. In a perfect, English accent it said: 'I presume that rather coarse whistle indicated that my services are required?'

Tiger seemed rather embarrassed – rather like someone at a posh dinner party who has been spotted eating peas off his knife. 'Well, yes – er – Hudson.' He sounded apologetic. 'I thought we'd take a ride on the new highway.'

'Certainly,' the car responded. 'Your voice print has been checked and the doors are now unlocked. Welcome aboard, Sir.'

'Hudson?' Mary asked, once they were settled into their seats and gliding smoothly along.

The Doctor explained. '*H*euristic *U*niversal *D*river with *S*ensory and *O*rbital Navigation.'

'Electronics by Hiro,' Mary guessed. It had all the trappings of the Japanese lieu tenant's genius for invention.

'Exactly,' Tiger smiled. 'Well, what do you think?'

Mary was in no doubt. 'It's beautiful.'

'I rather think, Madam,' said Hudson, a trifle snootily, 'that the question was addressed to me.' He transmitted his findings to Ninestein. 'The road is undoubtedly of superlative quality. The surface is smooth, but with good traction. Very advanced engineering, my opinion.'

The commander nodded, looking from side to side as they coasted along. Then his eye caught something – something very odd – just ahead. In the same instant, Hudson saw it too, and came to a nicely controlled stop. Lying by the side of the road were groups of cubes, for all the world like giant dice, or large parcels. Gifts, perhaps. Gifts from Zelda.

Mary peered out of her window at them. 'What are they?' she asked.

Ninestein smelled danger. 'I don't know,' he replied, 'but they look extremely dicey to me. Let's get out of here.'

Obediently, Hudson started forward; but before the car could travel more than a few feet, the cubes suddenly sprang to life, hurtling through the air and forming two pillars on either side of the highway, as if they were children's building blocks with minds of their own. Within a second, an amber-coloured forcefield transmitted from one pillar to the other. The way forward was barred.

Rapidly, Hudson switched to reverse. But more cubes had lined up on either side of the road behind them. There was a hiss as another forcefield closed behind them. Tiger yanked open his door. 'Run for it,' he yelled.

'Hiss! Hiss! Amber walls shot between the blocks, closing off the escape on either side. Tiger turned, to see Mary, her door half-open, gazing in dismay at the forcefield on her side of the car. 'I guess,' he remarked drily, 'that was obvious.'

Mary looked horrified. 'We're trapped,' she gasped.

'That's also obvious,' Ninestein agreed.

He pondered a moment, then gave an instruction. 'Try the laser, Hudson; though my theory is–' He paused, watching the silver lady on Hudson's bonnet retract, to be replaced by a Microzoid which sent out a fizzing laser beam. There came a fierce crackling sound, but the beam made no impact. '–That forcefield is impenetrable,' sighed Tiger.

Hudson confirmed. 'I'm afraid so, Sir.'

'Give me a satellite link.'

Hudson's radiator-grille moved forward, on mechanical struts, and angled skywards. Tiger gripped the onboard microphone. 'Calling all Terrahawks! This is a ten-ninety. A ten-ninety. We are trapped in an impenetrable forcefield. Stand by for instructions. In the meantime, make no attempt to rescue us.'

Before any Terrahawk could reply, the witch's croak that Ninestein had come to know so well broke in on his radio-link.

'*I* will not attempt to rescue you,' she mocked. 'You cannot escape. You are in your tomb.' From the Battlehawk, Sergeant-major Zero listened in horror to Zelda's transmission. 'And be sure of it,' gloated the evil android, 'you will both die!'

‘Oh, Doctor,’ moaned Zero, ‘why didn’t you believe me?’

Above the trapped car, Hawkwing circled and swooped. There was no way to help. The craft might have shattered the forcefield by ramming it – but then Hudson, and his passengers, would be shattered too. The forcefield would be self-generating, which meant in theory, it could remain there forever, long after Tiger and Mary had died of starvation. It *was* like being in a tomb ... like being buried alive. Without food and water, the victims could not expect to last long.

As she flew over the sight, Kate conferred anxiously with her gunnery officer. After a while, she flicked the switch on her communications panel.

‘Tiger – I’ve been talking to Hawkeye. We reckon we can drop supplies to you-‘ She had not finished speaking when she saw the final amber wall of forcefield close over the top of the Rolls-Royce.

Zelda chuckled. She had anticipated them – of course. ‘Your fate is *sealed,*’ she joked cruelly. ‘Goodbye, Doctor.’

Neither Mary nor Dr Ninestein spoke for a while. Then Mary, a rueful smile on her face, commented: ‘I hate to say it–’

'Then I will,' Tiger broke in. 'Zero was right. It's ironic, isn't it? He's the only one who can save us.'

Mary puzzled over this remark for a second, before realizing what the Doctor was getting at. Any attack on the forcefield by Terrahawk weaponry would destroy them along with the forcefield that held them captives. It would take something much less explosive – and much more selective and accurate – to free them without harm. Zero!

One of the sergeant-major's unique qualities was that he could increase his weight by a massive amount, without in any way altering shape, using the same principal that made any matter tremendously heavy when it was compressed. Stars, after they exploded and became only a tiny fraction of their previous size, obeyed the same natural law. Mary assumed that this was Ninestein's theory.

'By increasing his mass?' she asked.

'Yes,' the Doctor replied. 'He can make himself as heavy as a Black Hole. If he hit one of these posts,' and he waved a hand towards the piles of cubes that held the forcefield, 'he could break the field.'

Mary looked up at the amber sheet above them, blocking all radio communication. 'But we can't call him.'

Tiger's eyes followed the direction hers had taken. 'Not now,' he said ruefully.

'Maybe he'll think of it himself'

Ninestein doubted it. 'I told him that if he ever disobeyed one of my orders again, I'd have him taken apart.' The order, of course, had been: 'You're a robot; don't think for yourself.'

In the Terrahawk, Zero was summing up the situation, and busily thinking for himself. 'I can save Mary,' he reasoned; then, as an afterthought, 'and the Doctor. But I will not disobey an order.' His voice became resolute. 'I will *not* disobey an order. I *definitely* will not disobey an order.'

He hopped off his perch and started to roll towards the zeroidoor. 'The heck I won't!' Through the door he sped, out onto the jungle floor – and started rolling.

On the Hawkwing scanner, Captain Kate Kestrel spotted his move. 'Hawkeye,' she cried excitedly, 'do you see what I see?'

'I sure do,' came the jubilant reply. 'He's increasing his mass. I just hope he's a good pitcher – he could smash that car to pieces!' His weight increasing with every passing second, Zero tore through the jungle, taking a short-cut to the trapped car. He did not swerve to avoid obstacles but took the shortest route between two points: a straight line. Vast trees crashed to the ground as he ripped through them. A path of devastation lay behind him

Breathlessly, the Hawkwing crew watched.

'Come on, Zero,' Kate yelled.

The sergeant-major concentrated fiercely on increasing his weight together with his speed. 'Increasing mass,' he roared, as he neared his target. *'Increasing mass!'* His enormous density was irresistible. Nothing standing upright could keep such power at bay.

At unbelievable speed, Zero rocketed out onto the road. His mass fearfully multiplied, and cannoned directly into one of the pillars of cubes. A perfectly aimed strike! The cubes flew through the air. The forcefield was destroyed.

His mission accomplished, Zero rolled back to the Rolls-Royce. Captain Falconer was leaning out of her window, beaming. 'Fantastic, Sergeant-major! Just fantastic!'

Zero injected a note of modesty into his voice. 'It

was nothing, Ma'am … nothing.'

'You're right,' Ninestein muttered – *almost* to himself.

Mary turned on him. 'Tiger–' she began. Ninestein grinned and raised his hands in mock defence. 'joke,' he insisted. 'joke – it was just my little joke.'

The danger was over – for the time being at least. As they sped back towards the Battlehawk, Mary took the opportunity to check out a few of Hudson's specifications – and came to the conclusion that Tiger's 'Roller' was really something special.

'You know, Tiger,' she said, putting her thoughts in to words, 'Hudson is absolutely magnificent.'

As she spoke, the car seemed to react. Mary could see the bodywork changing colour, to become a deep, rich pink. 'Why, Hudson,' she said teasingly. 'I do believe you're blushing.'

'No, Madam,' Hudson assured her, 'it's my natural colour.'

'Pink?' asked Mary in astonishment. It seemed an unlikely colour for Tiger to have chosen.

'No, Madam,' came the reply. 'Chameleon.' And to emphasize the point, Hudson changed, in rapid order, from pink, to red, then to white, then to blue. He could, in fact, become any colour he chose, to suit a mood, to complement a lady's gown, or – more importantly – to camouflage himself in dangerous situations. Another miraculous piece of technical mastery from Lieutenant Hiro.

'Red, white and blue,' observed Mary. 'Truly British, Hudson. Truly British.'

Later that same night, the party in the White House had picked up where it had left off. Music and laughter could be heard; the lights were ablaze. Sergeant-major Zero, however, was not feeling very festive as he followed the Doctor into the Terrahawk. In fact, he had the uncomfortable notion that he was going to be 'put on the carpet'. He had done the wrong thing again, even if it had resulted in saving the lives of the commander and – just as important – the sergeant-major's beloved Captain Falconer.

Ninestein's voice was stern as he said, 'All right, Zero, up on your perch.' The zeroid hopped up, as he was bidden. 'Today,' Tiger continued, 'you disobeyed an order – once again. You started to think for yourself.'

'Yes, Sir, but––'

Ninestein cut him off. The anger in his voice became more pronounced. 'When are you going to realize that you were made – and programmed – by a superior being?'

As the commander paused for breath, Zero cut in. Something had just occurred to him, something he should have thought of long before. 'With due respect, Sir,' he commented, 'weren't you …' He could not quite bring himself to state the obvious. But, of course, he did not have to.

Tiger looked taken aback for an instant. Then he looked at the robot with something like respect. ‘Sergeant-major,’ he said thoughtfully, ‘maybe I’ve underestimated you.’

Mary Falconer, who had come to take Ninestein across to the party in the White House, had been standing in the doorway of the Terrahawk listening to every word. ‘*Now* perhaps he’ll understand,’ she thought. She knew that Zero’s devotion to his commander was immensely strong. More than anything, though, this zeroid – who *could* think for himself, who *did* have feelings – wanted Ninestein's admiration, wanted to prove that he, a robot, could act and *think* and *feel* like a man. Or like Tiger Ninestein: like a clone. Neither of them was truly human; but that didn't stop either having pride, feeling sorrow, showing courage.

Hearing Tiger’s words she felt a surge of happiness. Out loud, she merely said: ‘I never thought I’d see the day!’ Then, waving an arm in the direction of the lights and noise in the White House, she asked, ‘Coming?’

Zero watched as they left the Terrahawk. Then, a second later, a head popped back around the door. ‘Thanks, Zero,’ said Tiger Ninestein. The door closed.

There was silence for a full ten seconds. Then the sergeant-major bounded down from his perch in a victory leap of glee and bounced frantically about the room. ‘Thanks, Zero!’ he shouted. ‘*Thanks,* Zero!’ He bounced higher and more jubilantly. ‘Thanks, *Zero!*’ he crowed. ‘Yippee! Wow! Whoopee! Zap! Pow!’ And he bounced and bounced for sheer joy.

Chapter Four

The Terrahawks had proved themselves! In their first conflict with the new Martians they had defended Earth from a terrible enemy with all the bravery and daring that the UN High Command had expected. Zelda had been outfought and outwitted. For the time being, anyway- for the Terrahawks knew that her evil campaign was not over by any means.

Even though they had won, they had tasted something of her witch-like powers. They now knew her to be an evil and cunning foe – a foe who would not give up easily. Thanks to the elite fighting force, Earth was still free – but only just; and only until the next time!

Over the few days following Zero's dramatic rescue of Ninestein and Captain Falconer, the Unit stayed at all times on Alert, prepared for Zelda's next campaign. Every minute, every hour, they expected – the unexpected. And if they had been able to see what was going on in the Martian base, they would have witnessed something very unexpected indeed.

In the central hub of her own control complex on the Red Planet, Zelda was cowering pathetically. Cringing away from some menace, her repulsive features twisted in fear. When she spoke, her voice trembled with terror. 'You have beaten me, Doctor. I am powerless.'

Tiger Ninestein stood before her. Though he was victorious, his face was pale, his eyes lined with the dark shadows of fatigue. 'Powerless,' he agreed, 'powerless even to mend your evil ways, Zelda.' He advanced on her menacingly. 'I have no alternative—'

The android slunk back further, quaking with fright. 'Doctor!' she begged. 'Please—'

Ninestein's face was grave. 'No more chances Zelda. The earth will not be safe until you are gone – forever!'

'Pleas' she whimpered.

Tiger Ninestein shook his head firmly. 'The game is over, Zelda!'

'No!' she screamed. *'No!'*

'And so are you!'

Zelda looked up, filled with dread, at the figure of doom towering over her. For the space of two heartbeats, neither of them moved. Then there came the sound of wild applause and they both relaxed; Zelda cackled with glee, as two androids appeared from the shadows clapping their hands in delight. These were Yungstar and Cystar: Zelda's son and her sister. Both were as ugly as Zelda, both as evil; but neither of them possessed Zelda's powers or her slyness. They did, however, possess quirks of their own – in their warped android brains, they imagined themselves clever and brave. The truth was that Yungstar was, at heart, a craven coward. And as for Cystar! Zelda sometimes wondered whether she had a brain at all.

The pair clapped and clapped, anxious to please their leader. 'Wonderful! Wonderful!' they cried. And Yungstar, turning to Tiger, said, 'Bravo, Moid! Bravo!'

Zelda and Ninestein took their bows, like actors at the end of a play. Cystar applauded so violently that her wig (she was a vain android, as well as stupid) fell over her eyes.

Zelda looked pleased and excited. 'Excellent!' she screeched. Then, waving a hand towards the person next to her, she said, 'Was he not *excellent* as the disgusting clone, Ninestein?'

Yungstar dribbled on his chin in his eagerness to please. 'Yes, indeed,' he croaked. His voice burbled like bubbles of slime bursting in a polluted mud hole. 'How do you do it, Moid?'

Ninestein's double – the creature who had just been addressed as Moid – changed his voice from the crisp, level tones he had been using to imitate Tiger, and spoke in a perfect copy of Yungstar's disgusting warble. 'I have always had a small talent for mimicry.'

Cystar looked at Moid in amazement. 'That was your voice, Yungstar,' she simpered, fluffing out her ill-fitting wig. 'He is truly amazing.'

Yungstar looked outraged. 'I don't talk in that … that *stupid* way,' he insisted.

'You do.' Cystar sneered at him.

'I do not!'

Zelda shut them both up. 'Of course you do, you gurgling idiot.'

She smiled crookedly at the Ninestein lookalike. 'Our friend is too modest. His has no small talent. Years of dedication have made him, Moid, Master Of Infinite Disguise.'

Moid responded with a precise copy of Zelda's cracked and rasping tone. 'You are too kind to your humble servant,' he told her. Hearing their leader's voice coming from what appeared to be Ninestein's lips, Yungstar and Cystar shrieked with laughter.

'Be quiet!' screamed Zelda.

Instantly, the pair fell silent. They knew that when Zelda was angry, her vengeance could be terrible. The android leader glared at them for a moment. Then she said: 'Our plan is laid.'

'And I have a theory,' said Moid, using Tiger's voice, 'that it's going to work.'

This time it was Zelda who led the wild peals of crazy, raucous mirth.

Lieutenant Hawkeye settled himself in the chair that faced the Terrahawk control console. 'Okay, Tiger,' he said. 'If you want to see me beat you again … .' On the VDU was the video-game that

Ninestein had never quite managed to win. The computer-lettering read: Top Score 749. *I know I can beat that,* thought Tiger; *but there's always some interruption.* Time after time, he had come within an inch of that elusive 750. But it took a keen eye and a quick response to even get close. *Next time,* he told himself. But now he stood back, watching confidently, as Hawkeye pressed the button to start the game and gripped the control lever, his thumb hovering over the 'fire' trigger.

'I want to see you *try,*' he told Hawkeye, grinning.

On screen, the invaders came in at tree top height. Hawkeye started to pick them off. As Tiger watched the lieutenant's progress, he heard Mary Falconer report: 'Hiro is ready for lift-off in Treehawk.'

'Thanks, Mary,' said the commander, never once taking his eyes off the video-screen. Then: 'Hiro – have a good f*r*ight.'

Only Hiro appeared not to notice the joke. In response to Tiger's remark, he simply said, 'Ten-ten.'

Tiger watched as one of the zooming ships got past the electronic blip of Hawkeye's missile. 'You missed, Hawkeye' he chuckled. 'Maybe you're losing your touch.'

Three more invaders swept into view, skimming the skyline. Without hesitating,

Hawkeye brought them down – *Bam! Bam! Bam!* – in rapid succession. The score rattled up to 150. Ninestein began to look dismayed. 'And maybe you're not,' he conceded.

Nearby, Mary was giving Hiro clearance for take-off 'Treehawk,' she advised, 'you have a ten-fifty.'

'Ten-ten.'

On the surface, there was a rumbling of heavy machinery as the tree that formed part of Hiro's launch-path separated into spokes and fell back. A second later, the shuttle, with Hiro at the controls, erupted from the earth on its way back to the orbiting Spacehawk. The lieutenant was heading back to his solitary look-out post in deep space, back to Space Sergeant 101 and Hiro's beloved collection of house plants.

Once she was satisfied that Hiro's lift-off had gone smoothly, Mary turned her attention to Ninestein, and to Hawkeye who was still crouched over the controls of the video-game. She wanted to remind them about a rather special event: something she had been looking forward to since UN Command had told about it. She tracked a radio- impulse on her scanner and switched to full visual monitoring. The inky depths of space, littered with stars, came up on the screen.

'Excuse me, gentlemen,' said Mary, 'but we should be getting our first sight of Bell's comet any minute now.'

Ninestein's eyes remained glued to the VDU, where Hawkeye's. score was mounting with alarming rapidity. He said, 'Uh-huh.'

Mary sounded affronted. 'You don't seem very interested in a comet that has only passed within terrestrial range *once* before—' she emphasized the date, '–in 1328.'

'Uh-huh,' muttered Ninestein. To Hawkeye, he said: 'You missed that one, hot-shot.'

'*Men!*' exclaimed Mary, in exasperation.

There came a discreet cough from where Sergeant-major Zero sat on his perch at the back of the Terrahawk. Captain Falconer smiled. 'Excepting you, Sergeant-major.'

The zeroid wobbled with pride. 'Thank you, Ma'am.'

Mary went back to tracking the approach of the comet, leaving Ninestein and Hawkeye to their competition. Her screen showed nothing as yet, so she decided to seek a little more detailed information from the crew of Spacehawk.

She selected the appropriate frequency. 'Space Sergeant?'

'Yes, Captain Falconer.' The zeroid, who controlled the Unit's space station while Hiro was on a trip to earth, had already been advised of the Captain's interest in the approaching comet. Linked to the Spacehawk's computer, 101 could monitor the comet's approach from the vantage-point of space.

'Do we have a track yet?' Mary wanted to know.

'It's coming into range now,' replied 101. 'The comet will be visible in the eastern sky for one and a half minutes.'

Mary kept her eyes riveted to the screen. There came a faint glow, lighting the very edge of the space sky and then – gloriously, spectacularly – the comet came into view, blazing across the limitless wastes of outer space, a tremendous glowing ball of gases and particles, with its brilliant tail streaking behind it over millions and millions of miles of the universe.

Mary gazed at it in wonder and almost missed 101's next remark. 'I'm getting a double echo on the scanner,' the zeroid reported.

Mary sprang out of her reverie. 'Check!' she ordered.

There was a gap of a second or two. Then the space sergeant's voice said: 'Confirmed. It *is* a double echo.'

Mary knew it could mean only one thing. Something else was up there; something they could not see; something that was using Bell's comet as cover; something that wanted to remain hidden. And that meant something dangerous, something sly. Zelda!

The VDU showed an astronomical score – and Hawkeye was still shooting: bringing down one invader after another.

Mary interrupted: 'Tiger, we have a problem. I'm calling a ten-forty.'

Ninestein had been so engrossed in the game that he had not been aware of what was going on elsewhere in the Terrahawk. But as soon as he heard Mary use the words 'ten-forty', he came alert. 'I'll be right there,' he told her, reaching across and snapping off the video-game. Hawkeye watched in dismay as the picture faded – and his score with it. Ninestein had trouble keeping the delight out of his voice as he said, 'Pleasure before business, Hawkeye.'

But it was business – Terrahawks business – that they were likely to be involved in soon, thought the lieutenant. 'Don't you mean—'

Ninestein grinned in a self-satisfied way. 'No,' he insisted. 'The way you were scoring, turning that thing off was a *pleasure.*'

Hawkeye made to leave. 'Underneath that craggy exterior,' he growled to himself, 'beats a heart of steel!'

Ninestein joined Mary Falconer at the control console. She was communicating with 101 on the Spacehawk. 'Report, Space Sergeant.'

‘The comet is still on course, but the echo is shifting. It’s moving away from the main body.’

Coming out into the open, thought Tiger. *Well, it couldn’t hide for ever: the comet would only provide cover for a while, until it sped off on its endless route from galaxy to galaxy.*

‘Identify – fast!’ he said.

‘Ten-ten.’ The space sergeant watched the visual display as the comet streamed past. As it began to pass out of Spacehawk’s sector of observation, a space ship emerged from the blur of the tail and banked away on a new course. Almost immediately, hatch-doors opened and a smaller craft – fast and built for intricate manoeuvring – left the main ship. The zeroids in Spacehawk’s hull spotted it and registered the information with their central computer.

‘Positive identification,’ said 101. ‘It’s a ZEAF.’

These small, racy ships had been monitored by UN Spacewatch as they flew to and fro above the Martian surface. It was clear that they were designed for battle at low altitudes – well inside the ionosphere. For that reason, they had been dubbed Zelda Earth Atmospheric Fighters: or ZEAFs.

Ninestein did not wait to hear more. ‘Lock onto ZEAF,’ he commanded.

‘Ten-ten,’ said 101. ‘Locking on.’

Mary watched the action with some concern. She would have been a great deal happier if Hiro had been aboard the Spacehawk. Not that she did not trust 101 to obey orders to the letter. But she valued more the lieutenant's sharp brain and his coolness under pressure.

Just at that moment, Hiro's voice broke in to the radio contact. Treehawk had been on the point of levelling its flight-path to home in on Spacehawk's trajectory, when he had noticed a strange signal on his radar screen. Some unidentified ship had appeared and was closing fast. 'I've got something on the scanner,' he told the Terrahawk. 'It's coming straight for me.'

Mary replied. 'We've got it, Hiro. It's a ZEAF. Spacehawk's locked on.'

Ninestein tracked the two trajectories and made a quick computation. There was not much time. To 101, he said, 'Open fire as soon as you can.'

'Targeting now,' came the response.

Hiro, Mary and Tiger watched apprehensively as the ZEAF zoomed in on Treehawk: a blip on their scanners, narrowing the gap second by second.

'Dr Ninestein!' 101's voice was filled with alarm.

'You're running out of time, 101,' the Doctor interrupted. The order had been given to fire at will. What was making the zeroid hesitate?

‘I can't fire, Sir. Treehawk will be caught in the detonation.’

Mary’s face grew pale. She realized that Hiro was on his own now. The two blips on the scanner in front of her had almost merged into one.

‘Hiro,’ snapped the commander. ‘ZEAF closing. Take evasive action.’ It was the only hope.

Hiro flipped the computer-control to ‘Evade’ and gave it a bearing on the approaching ZEAF. Instantly Treehawk banked, increasing speed. As if attached by a tow-line, the pursuer tilted, following the same course, and gave chase.

‘It’s right on my tail,’ cried Hiro despairingly. ‘Closing fast.’ Through the pitch-black space sky, the two ships roared on a twisting, looping course at furious speeds, their photon-drive engines streaking the darkness with trails of white and orange flame. Hiro’s fingers raced over the computer controls as he tried desperately to shake off his enemy; but the ZEAF was built for this kind of warfare. Treehawk – a space shuttle built for work – was no match for the lethal ZEAF. As Hiro came out of a steep dive, and levelled off for the briefest of moments, the hunter saw its prey in the sights and loosed an energy-bolt. ‘I’ve suffered a strike,’ Hiro informed Tiger. ‘Main thrusters ten-zero.’

The frantic chase had taken Treehawk and the ZEAF to the very edge of Earth's atmosphere. Now, with his main thrusters out of action, Hiro felt the space shuttle stall, hang for a moment as if suspended by a giant hawser, then begin to dive, as the faintest pull of gravity took hold. He wrestled with the controls, punching program after program into the computer. Nothing worked. The computer, like the main thrusters, was dead.

Treehawk travelled faster and faster as its dive took it back into the atmosphere and into the grip of gravity. Just behind him, perfectly controlled, the ZEAF followed.

Tiger watched as the Treehawk dived earthwards, its speed increasing with every passing second. 'Hiro,' he yelled, 'can you hear me?'

The lieutenant's voice was very faint. 'Just about, Dr Ninestein.' They were losing radio-contact! 'The ZEAF's still on your tail,' Ninestein shouted.

The space shuttle was pointing straight down now, and coming close to terminal velocity. At the controls, Hiro was being battered by crushing centrifugal forces. Waves of blackness swept before his eyes; there was a drumming in his ears. Gradually – but surely – he was losing consciousness. Pieces of fuselage started to fly into the air, stripping off from the place where the energy-bolt had struck.

Frantically, Ninestein flicked the communications switch. ‘Hiro - come in. Hiro, do you read me?’

Hiro’s voice was strained; a mere whisper. Tiger could barely hear him, but he could tell that the lieutenant was virtually out for the count. ‘I … read … you … Doctor.’

Hold on Hiro. Ninestein willed the Spacehawk commander to stay conscious. *Hold on!*

‘Hiro,’ he roared the words out, ‘you’re in a vertical crash-dive at sixty thousand feet. You must activate the auxiliary motors.’

Through the fog that was enveloping him, Hiro heard the instruction and struggled to carry it out. Summoning his last reserves of strength, he reached across the control panel and found the switch. He pressed it. 'Activating motors––’

But Terrahawk’s underground central control unit knew that Hiro's decelerating action could lead to Treehawk plunging erratically – fatally – round an increasing centrifugal spiral. Inevitably, as Treehawk’s kinetic power lessened, ultimate metal torsion began. Zero, who was monitoring Hiro’s descent, cut in. ‘Forty-five thousand feet,’ he warned.

‘Speed?’ Mary Falconer queried.

‘Slowing, but still critical, Ma’am.’

Now Tiger took over again. 'Hiro, we've computed the damage status on Treehawk. You're going to have to fly her manually.' It was the only way of preventing the craft from braking up.

The auxiliary motors had done enough to slow the ship and reduce the G-forces that were tearing at the lieutenant. His voice was stronger now, more in control. 'Ten-ten,' he said, 'switching to manual.' Still Treehawk plummeted earthwards, as Hiro wrestled with the manual flying gear. The retractable wings in the fuselage folded outwards, as part of manual operation technique.

'Twenty thousand feet.' Zero sounded panicky.

'For space *sake,*' muttered Ninestein to himself, 'level out!'

Hiro fought for control of the ship, sweat standing out on his brow. Slowly – agonisingly slowly – Treehawk began to respond, the nose of the ship rising inch by inch. Finally, Hiro could glimpse the horizon. The ship began to respond more and more, until its flight-path became a shallow curve.

'Treehawk in controlled descent,' Hiro reported.

'He's done it!' Mary exclaimed. Relief was plain on her face – and on Ninestein's. He realized, though, that the lieutenant was not completely safe yet. The crazy course of his unplanned descent had taken him hundreds of miles off route - that, and the distance he had covered when trying to escape from the ZEAF. It was hard to say how much damage Treehawk had suffered; but one thing was clear. The shuttle would have been fairly low on fuel by the time it broke through the earth's atmosphere and set a course for Spacehawk; normally it carried just a little more than was needed for the trip. With the chase and the extra bum needed for the auxiliary motors, there would be precious little left.

The first move was to organize a rescue operation. ‘Launching Hawkwing,’ Ninestein told Mary.

‘Hawkwing,’ she said into her console-mike, ‘you have a ten-fifty.’

Kate Kestrel activated the photon-drive. ‘Ten-ten.’ Hawkwing screamed along its launch tunnel towards the sea-doors, then 'through into the lake's vortex, and away.

In Treehawk, there was no roar of engines. As Ninestein had thought, the mad dash through space had resulted in the ship being, now, without drive power. Hiro reported the fact. ‘I’m out of fuel,’ he said, looking out for a suitable landing-site. The Treehawk glided silently on for a minute or so, tracked by the Terrahawk. Ahead, the lieutenant could see a vast, white expanse of frozen tundra. ‘I’m approaching an ice-field. I’ll ditch there.’

‘Ten-ten,’ said Ninestein, adding the reassuring information: ‘Hawkwing’s on its way.’

Hiro lined his craft up for a crash-landing on the fast approaching waste of snow and ice. He tried to judge his line of approach to find the best terrain; but he realized that there was no knowing what lay beneath the blanket of snow. It all looked level enough, but it was impossible to predict whether or not rocks and crevasses lurked just below the surface.

He picked his spot, mentally crossed his fingers, and touched down. The Treehawk flopped, became airborne again for a second, then came down hard on the surface, skittering and slithering on the hard-packed ice. There was nothing Hiro could do to control the bucking ship. He just sat tight as it skidded over boulders and concealed dips in the ground, heading straight for a rockpile by a sheer cliff-face. He shielded his face, steeling himself for the impact. The ship ploughed into the boulders at terrific speed and came to a shuddering halt.

‘He's down.’ Mary was peering intently at the VDU, checking the location of Hiro’s radar impulse. In Hawkwing, Kate was seeing the same picture.

‘We have the crash coordinates,’ she radioed. ‘We’ll be there in thirty minutes.’

When he came to, Hiro was only aware of the intense cold. The cockpit hatch on Treehawk had flown off on impact: a standard safety procedure; but it had resulted in Hiro being exposed to the sub-zero temperatures on the ice-field. The next thing he noticed, though, was even more alarming: a smell of fuel. It was clear that although the tiny puddle in the tanks had not been enough to get into Treehawk’s feed-line, there had been sufficient left to bleed into the cabin when the ship had crashed into the rock pile. *Tanks must have fractured,* thought Hiro, *must get out of here.*

Using all his strength, he levered himself out of the ship and over the side, falling heavily onto the frozen snow beneath. He lay there for a moment, dazed; then he spotted a cave in the rock face. Pushing himself to his feet, he began a wavering journey towards it, falling now and then – sometimes because of the concussion he had suffered during the crash, sometimes because his feet slipped from under him on the ice.

Finally, he made it to the mouth of the cave. Like the white world outside, it was frozen over – the walls carrying a thick coat of ice. *At least it’s out of the wind,* Hiro thought. He found a ledge and crashed down on it, barely conscious. Ice particles began to form on his eyebrows and hair. His eyes closed. The last thing he heard before he lapsed into oblivion, was the sighing of the freezing wind at the mouth of the cave.

He came to with a start, not knowing how long he had been lying there. For a moment, he did not register what it was that had reached his sleeping senses and brought him awake so sharply. He glanced towards the entrance to the cave, then spun round as the sound that had woken him came again. A footfall! Coming from the dark depths behind him.

'Who's there?' He released the energy-bolt gun from his belt and gripped the handle tightly. There was no reply to his question - just silence. Then there came another footfall. Hiro levelled the gun, pointing it at the shadows. 'Who is it?" he demanded. 'Identify yourself.' From the gloom, a figure began to emerge, unspeaking, stealthy. 'Stop, or I fire!'

'Hold your fire.'

I know that voice, thought Hiro. He said: 'Dr Ninestein?'

The figure stepped into the light from the mouth of the cave. 'Yes, it's me.' Hiro gasped a sigh of relief and lowered his gun. Before him stood Ninestein, dressed for the cold in a cloak and fur hat. He seemed pale and his eyes were dark with tiredness. *The tension of the last encounter must have taken it out of him,* thought Hiro. In his confused state, the lieutenant did not stop to wonder how Ninestein had managed to reach him before Hawkwing. 'Doctor,' he breathed, 'am I glad to see you!'

'I am pleased to have found you,' came the response.

'There was a fire hazard in Treehawk,' Hiro went on,' – fuel spillage. I thought I'd better get clear.'

'Very wise.'

As Ninestein came closer, Hiro noticed again how ashen his face was, how ringed with shadow his eyes.

'Doctor, are you feeling all right?' he asked.

'Nothing to worry about, Hiro. But you look in bad shape.'

'I'm fine,' Hiro told him bravely. 'Not a scratch.'

The commander took a small case out from the folds of his cloak and unsnapped the catch. Inside lay a full medical kit.

'You *will* be fine,' Tiger said. 'I'll give you something for the shock.' He removed a syringe and a bottle of serum from the case. Hiro looked at it, warily. He did not terribly like injections.

'If you think it's necessary,' he said.

'I do. Roll up your sleeve.'

Hiro laughed weakly and did as he was bidden.

'You're the doctor.' He flinched a little as the needle entered his arm. Almost immediately, he felt a sensation of giddiness. There was a drumming in his ears. Black, oily waves of light seemed to sweep up from the cave door, obscuring the glass-like walls of ice. *Something for the shock?* he thought dimly. He struggled to stand up, but could not do more than lift his head. Ninestein's pale face swam in and out of focus. Hiro seemed to be seeing him through a haze, his features falling apart. Then the drumming grew louder and the black fog grew thicker. And in another second, he was out like a light.

'Ice has a cold serenity, don't you think?' asked

Moid. He knew that Hiro could not hear him. Bending over, he passed a hand in front of the lieutenant's eyes. There was no response. 'A cold serenity …' Moid repeated. Then he began to laugh: crazed, jagged shrieks of mirth that bounced off the ice walls and echoed madly through the cave. Zelda's laugh.

Kate Kestrel set Hawkwing down neatly, just a few yards from the grounded space shuttle. Quickly, they left their craft and began a search of the area. A rapid glance into the cockpit of

Treehawk let them know that Hiro had found some other shelter – and when she smelled the fuel, Katie could tell why. They found the cave almost at once and went inside.

'Over there!' Hawkeye followed Kate's pointing finger and saw a shape huddled on a ledge. They had not arrived a minute too soon, he thought. Hiro's legs were almost covered by powdery snow that had blown in through the cave door. His face and hair were glistening with frost. His eyes were closed.

Hawkeye stode over to where the inert lieutenant lay. 'Hiro, can you hear me?' Kate, looking over Hawkeye's shoulder, saw Hiro's eyes open and scan their faces. She was not sure, though, how well he could see them.

'Let's get him to Hawkwing,' she said. Together, they carried Hiro to the ship and installed him in the 'egg'; Kate climbed in alongside and began to wind up the engines. In a great billow of powdered snow and ice, Hawkwing climbed away from the desolate scene and set a course for the White House.

Zelda's mother-ship had long since recovered the ZEAF and returned to the base on Mars, looking back into the complex of ships that made up the Martian 'city'. Crouched over her tracking-screen, Zelda laughed horribly; her gluey eyes shone with delight. Nearby, Yungstar and Cystar watched her, also cackling softly.

'So,' Zelda crowed, 'our plan nears completion. We can prepare to launch the final attack.'

'The final attack?' Yungstar burbled.

'Yes – with every ship in our fleet.' *This time,* thought the ugly android, *this time Dr Tiger Ninestein … the victory shall be mine.*

'An attack!' Cystar simpered gleefully. Then a thought struck her, and a look of puzzlement crossed her repellent face. 'What shall I wear? A new dress?'

Zelda sneered and raised her eyes in exasperation. 'A dress?' she croaked angrily. Cystar really was a hopelessly feather-brained android. 'You need an attire suitable for battle.'

'Of course,' Cystar cried, 'a *battledress!*'

Zelda ignored her. 'I shall be clad–– ' she leered at the prospect, '– I shall be clad – in Victory!'

Now that Hiro had been returned to HQ, the atmosphere in the Hawknest was a great deal more relaxed. Sergeant-major Zero watched as Ninestein added some information to the computer. The zeroid was mumbling to himself, happily and bouncing gently on his perch. He seemed mildly excited.

By the time Tiger had completed his computing, Zero's antics had begun to grate on his nerves.

‘Zero, what are you–’ Tiger searched for a word that would describe the zeroid’s expression, *‘–grinning* about?’

The sergeant-major sounded both pleased and bashful when he said: ‘It's – er – it’s my birthday, Sir.’

Tiger looked at him in blank amazement. ‘Your *what?*’

‘Birthday, Sir.’ Zero gave a couple of extra bounces. ‘I checked on my date of manufacture. I was switched on, for the very first time, four years ago today. At 04.00 hours, to be precise.’

Ninestein clapped a hand to his forehead. When *would* this zeroid begin to understand that he wasn’t a man – wasn't human? ‘I don't believe this,’ he exclaimed. ‘Zero, you weren’t born, you were *made.* Get it?’

Zero sounded crestfallen. But he knew better than to argue. He simply said, ‘Got it, Sir.’

No he hasn’t, thought Ninestein, *he never will.* ‘Get out of here,’ he said irritably.

‘Sir!’ Zero bounced towards the door, passing Lieutenant Hiro as he went.

Ninestein looked up, pleased to see the lieutenant back on his feet so soon. ‘Hiro; how are you?’

‘I'm fine, Doctor. I’d like to get back on duty.’

Tiger regarded him. He certainly gave every appearance of being completely fit again. Still, concussion could be a funny thing. ‘Well, if you feel up to it.’ The commander decided it was best to leave the decision to Hiro.

‘Yes,’ the lieutenant insisted. ‘I want to get back to Spacehawk.’

Tiger knew how loyal and dedicated Hiro was; it would be just like him to want to resume his duties as soon as he possibly could. That eagerness, that loyalty, was just one of the many reasons that had made Ninestein select Hiro to be one of the Terrahawks; together with his genius for technical detail and his ability to remain calm in the kind of crisis he had faced recently. There were one or two details of that crisis, though, that Tiger wanted to be sure about.

‘Are you certain that alien ship crashed?’ he queried.

Hiro nodded. As soon as he had been able to make his report, he had told how the ZEAF had failed to pull out of its dive as it followed him earthwards. After he had pulled himself clear, his report went, he had seen the ship out of control and on course for destruction.

‘Straight into a glacier,’ he confirmed. ‘Anyone aboard would have been killed instantly.’

Ninestein mulled this over for a moment. Then, coming to a decision, he said: ‘All right, Hiro. Get back on duty.’ As the lieutenant made to leave, he added, 'Give my regards to those plants of yours.'

Hiro hesitated, looking puzzled. Then he said, 'Yes – yes I will.'

101 was looking forward to having his chief back on board. His sensors detected the Treehawk docking with the bigger craft. The airlock hissed and then closed. Seconds later, Hiro stepped onto the flight-deck. If the space sergeant could have beamed, he would have. They were a team – he and the lieutenant. It was well-known that zeroids could not have feelings or, at least, it was assumed! But when he thought of himself as a part of the Terrahawks force – the force that defended Earth from alien attack, the zeroid experienced something that a human would have called pride. And now, as Hiro joined him in Spacehawk's central control area, there was something like pleasure – something very like it – coursing through his electrical circuits.

'Welcome back, Lieutenant,' he said.

Hiro did not respond. He walked straight to the control console, his spectacles pushed up on his forehead as if they were an annoyance to him. Without bothering to look at 101, he said, 'As of now, you will assume control of all operations on this ship.'

'Yes Lieutenant,' the zeroid replied obediently. Even so, the order puzzled and confused him. Of course he was more than able to take control of things. Every time Hiro made a journey to the Terrahawks base, 101 was left in charge.

He was specially programmed to deal with the technology of Spacehawk – and specially programmed, too, for the kind of unforeseen emergency the ship might have to face. It was 101 who was the first link with the ship's computer, monitoring the extra-terrestrial activity that occurred during their orbit through the star-studded endlessness of space. And he was the first line of command to the zeroid unit on board.

Oh, yes, he could pilot the ship all right; obey orders from headquarters; take the correctly computed action in a crisis. But he never assumed control of that sort when Hiro was aboard. Hiro was the Spacehawk commander.

101 was not at all sure – under the circumstances – of just what 'controlling all operations' involved.

'Yes Lieutenant,' he said again. Then: 'Does that mean–'

Hiro cut in, snappily. 'And you will obey no other instruction than my vocal command.'

'I control the ship and obey only your voice,' said the zeroid.

Hiro nodded. 'Exactly.'

The space sergeant's circuits almost fused in astonishment. ‘Sir!’ he exclaimed. ‘You said it!’

‘Said what?’ It was Hiro's turn to look puzzled.

‘Exact*l*y.’

‘Exactly,’ the lieutenant agreed, adding: ‘I’m going on a tour of inspection – the whole ship.’ He turned to leave; and as he did so, he noticed the array of house plants, their thick foliage spilling out into the control area.

‘Get those plants out of here,’ he ordered angrily.

‘They're dust traps.’

For the second time in a minute, 101’s electrics went almost haywire. After Hiro had left, the sergeant began to search his memory banks frantically. But he did not really need confirmation of what he already knew. ‘Dust traps! *Dust traps!?*’ He remembered Hiro's affection for the plants: the loving care he gave to them; the fact that when he was on Earth, he always left strict instructions with 101 that he should talk to the plants so that they would not feel lonely. Even Commander Ninestein would pull the lieutenant’s leg about his devotion to them. ‘Dust traps,’ he said again. ‘Something’s wrong. Something’s terribly wrong.’

Zero bounced into the Terrahawk control to find Captain Mary Falconer checking some VDU readouts. He seemed upset, muttering darkly to himself, *'You weren't born, you were made.'* Ninestein's words had upset him. He jumped up onto his perch, still mumbling. 'Made, not born … made.' Then an idea came to him – a cheering idea. If you were not born, then you could not have a birthday – naturally. But that did not mean you could not celebrate. Celebrate what? Well, the day on which you were made, of course.

Bouncing gently on his perch, he began to sing, quietly. 'Happy Madeday to me, Happy Madeday to me––'

Mary Falconer had heard all about Zero's anniversary. With a chuckle in her voice, she asked: 'Am I to conclude that this is a day for celebration, Sergeant-major?'

Zero spoke proudly. 'Yes, Ma'am. The fourth anniversary of my day of manufacture.'

Mary smiled at him. 'Well, congratulations. Happy Madeday.'

If zeroids could have blushed with pleasure, Zero's face would have been bright pink. 'Thank you Ma'am.' Turning round to hide his glee, the sergeant-major increased his delighted bouncing.

'She's beautiful. She's made my day–' Then, realizing what he had said, he began to giggle uncontrollably. 'Made my day,' he chortled. 'Made my Madeday.'

In her command ship on the Red Planet, Zelda was feeling gleeful, too; though her happiness at the prospect of finally annihilating the Terrahawks fleet would have been greater if she had not had to watch the antics of her slovenly son and scatter-brained sister. Yungstar was taking his lunch-break, spooning mouthfuls of a disgusting black gooey substance into his dribbling mouth.

Zelda knocked the spoon away. Yungstar gurgled in annoyance. 'Leave that, you gluttonous wretch,' hissed Zelda.

Yungstar cowered resentfully. 'Carbon jelly,' he whined, 'my favourite.'

'The fleet is prepared,' said Zelda, ignoring him.

At that point, Cystar carne out of the shadows.

She was prancing and preening herself, showing off her 'battle dress'. On top of her lopsided wig, she wore a ridiculous, plumed helmet. An armoured breastplate was strapped crookedly over a party dress.

'Is this suitable for battle?' she croaked.

'Great mounds of dust,' said Yungstar. His voice resembled poisoned gas bubbling through liquid tar.

'What do you think?' Cystar simpered.

'I daren't tell you.'

Zelda had no time for this stupidity. There were more important matters to attend to.

‘Yes, it’s very nice dear,’ she said acidly. Then: ‘But now to the business in hand. Launch the fleet. Let battle be joined!’

First Zelda’s ship, then the others in the alien fleet, lifted off from the Martian surface, their destination – Earth. Their mission – to kill. To destroy.

Between them and their target, stood the awesome defences of the Spacehawk. But Zelda was not worried about that. She was not worried at all.

Sergeant-major Zero listened in amazement as 101 relayed his strange message. ‘It’s Lieutenant Hiro,’ he had begun.

At first, Zero had been only mildly puzzled. Why should the space sergeant be making a report about his superior? ‘Oh yes,’ he had said, ‘what about the lieutenant?’ Then came the bombshell.

‘I can’t explain it, but I think Lieutenant Hiro … isn’t Lieutenant Hiro!’

The words were no sooner out of his mouth, than a stern voice behind him said: ‘Space Sergeant!’ 101 whirled round. Hiro had returned and was confronting him angrily. At some point during his tour of inspection, he had abandoned his spectacles completely. There were dark shadows under his eyes; his face was ashen.

‘You will not contact Hawknest in any way. Is that understood?’

101 looked closely at Hiro. *Something ... something did not compute.* ‘Exactly,’ he had said. ‘Exact*l*y.’

And: ‘Those plants are dust traps.’ He was not wearing the thick spectacles that were so much a part of the lieutenant’s appearance. And his face … those dark shadows, the pale cheeks. It was wrong. It was all terribly wrong. 101’s circuits buzzed. But all he said was, ‘Yes, Lieutenant.’

Feeling somewhat embarrassed, Zero reported the strange message to Dr. Ninestein. ‘He must be sick, Sir – probably needs scrapping. But that’s what he said: Lieutenant Hiro wasn’t Lieutenant Hiro. *Ridiculous,*’ he added.

Ninestein thought carefully. There had been a number of things that had not added up. The impact of the ZEAF on the glacier had not registered on the control VDU. Of course there could have been an obstruction, or a fault in the radar. But then, Hiro’s recovery had been so fast and his desire to get back on duty in Spacehawk so strong. And the plants … It might have been a result of the concussion, but it had seemed to Ninestein that when he had mentioned the plants, *Hiro* had seemed – well – confused. All little things; none of them very suspicious on their own. But put them together, and ... .

Ridiculous? 'Maybe not,' Tiger said. He turned to the console mike. 'Kate, this is a ten-fifty for Hawkwing. I want you to search for the wreckage of the alien ship that Hiro said crashed on the glacier.'

Captain Kate Kestrel started Hawkwing along the launch tunnel. 'Ten-ten,' she said.

Almost as soon as Hawkwing was airborne, Zelda's fleet came within range of the Spacehawk's scanners. Receiving an impulse from the computer, 101 extended his antenna.

'Lieutenant – I have a contact.' He paused to compute the size of the signal. 'It looks like Zelda's entire fleet!'

'Thank you 101.' Hiro showed no emotion. Nor did it seem that he was going to do anything about the approaching ships. 101 knew that there was standard procedure for a moment like this.

'We should lock on and target,' he advised.

Hiro's voice was sharp with anger. 'Don't tell me what to do!'

In the rose garden outside the White House, the statue revolved, pointing its radar dish to the skies. Mary Falconer checked and double-checked her VDU screen. Then she turned to Ninestein, a worried frown creasing her forehead.

'We're picking up a massive signal. Spacehawk *must* have it.'

Tiger was not surprised. 'We have to assume that

Hiro is … some kind of replica.' He contacted the space sergeant directly. '101, this is Ninestein. I'm giving you a direct order. Open fire!'

101 swivelled on his perch in total confusion.

'You will obey no other instruction than my vocal

command,' Hiro had told him. And Hiro was his direct superior on Spacehawk. But Ninestein … .

'You obey only my command,' Hiro said.

'Fire immediately,' Ninestein ordered.

For the third time that day, 10l's circuits threatened to blow. Two commanders. Two orders. Two *opposing* orders. A zeroid was programmed to obey. But how could he obey both? His electrics heated.

'Obey,' he squawked hopelessly. 'Orders ... obey … master and slave … robots must … humans must … must be obeyed.' He whirled on his perch. A thin plume of smoke began to seep from his casing. 'Confused … obey … confused … fused … ten-zero … zero—' Then there was silence.

'He's shorted out, Sir. Shorted out—' Zero bellowed. Zelda's fleet, hurtling through space, grew nearer.

The android screeched in triumph. 'The Spacehawk is neutralized. Ninestein and his sniveling pack are at our mercy.' Yungstar and Cystar joined in her hysterical, insane laughter.

Mary Falconer's fingers flew over the computer buttons, but received no response. Spacehawk was non-operational. Ninestein looked anxiously at her, but she shook her head. 'The space zeroids are programmed to fire on a command from Space Sergeant 101,' she reminded him.

'And with 101 out of commission, we're in deep trouble.' Ninestein was watching the approach of the alien ships.

'Sir! There might be a way.'

Tiger turned in his seat to look at Zero, who was bouncing with eagerness. *Anything* , he thought, *I'll try anything.* 'Go ahead,' he rapped.

'Sir!'

In deep space, the zeroids listened to the voice of their sergeant-major. They listened … but they were programmed to respond *only* to Zeroid 101. Zero was going to have to think of some way of overriding that. Some way of appealing to the zeroid's feelings … the feelings they were not supposed to have!

'This is Sergeant-major Zero calling 101 and all you lovely space zeroids,' he began. 'You all know me, lads, and today is my Madeday.'

Not that again, Ninestein thought. *Not now!* he said: 'Get on with it, Zero.'

'Sir! Now I've never lied to you lads. In fact, I'm programmed not to lie.' He lowered his voice a fraction. 'But as we all know, there are ways round that particular circuit.'

'Zero!' yelled Ninestein furiously. Mary Falconer shot him a warning glance. She *could* see what Zero was up to. He was getting the zeroids on his side – talking to them like the loyal, brave troops he knew them to be. Talking to them like men!

He went on: 'What I mean is – I would never deceive any one of you. Zelda is launching a massive attack. And I want you to'' he waited for a second, then, at the top of his voice, roared, **'OPEN FIRE!'**

'*Hold* your fire!' Hiro's voice came like a whiplash.

The zeroids buzzed and muttered. Two orders … two officers.

'Men, the honour of the regiment is at stake. A regiment I am proud to lead … *proud* to *lead.*' Zero was giving it everything he had got. He detected a flicker of a response in 101's over-strained circuits.

'Sound the bugle,' shouted Zero. 'Let the tunes of glory ring in your ears!'

Summoning every trace of remaining electrical power, 101 said: 'I'm … with you …

Zero.' Hiro turned in alarm, opening his mouth to countermand any order 101 might give. The zeroid's casing opened and his EBG shot out, covering the lieutenant … *Moid.*

'Stay right where you are,' he cautioned. Then, to the zeroids, he said: 'This is Space Sergeant 101 … **OPEN FIRE**!'

A great cheer rang out from the row of zeroids in the Spacehawk's hull. Immediately, they loosed a deadly barrage of energy bolts at the fast dosing alien fleet. The space sky was suddenly alight with flame and tearing explosions.

Zelda's ship took a direct hit, the impact sending it veering off course. Inside, Yungstar and Cystar squealed in terror as they were thrown off-balance by the impact. Cystar's ridiculous helmet fell over her eyes.

'You told us we would be safe,' gargled Yungstar, as another terrific detonation flung the ship violently sideways. It was like being in the middle of an earthquake. Cystar clutched at her wig and wailed.

'Retreat. *Retreat!*' Yungstar shrieked.

Zelda clenched her fists in rage. 'I curse you, Ninestein,' she raved. She was beaten. She had been outwitted once more. 'Turn the fleet around,' she wailed.

There was jubilation in the Terrahawks' base as the radar signals showed Zelda's ships in full flight. Mary Falconer, for one, wanted to give praise where praise was due. Sergeant-major – you were marvellous.'

'He should get a medal,' Ninestein commented.

Zero tried his best to sound modest. 'A medal, Sir? Oh … I don't think I deserve it.'

Tiger looked at him in surprise. 'Not you, Zero. I'm talking about 101. He really saved the situation.'

'101? But …' Zero was outraged. But before he could get any further, Kate Kestrel's voice cut in.

'We're flying over the glacier,' she said. 'The ZEAF didn't crash.' It was as Ninestein had expected. But there was more to report. 'Our scan indicates one human life form in the area.'

'It has to be Hiro,' breathed Ninestein. 'The *real* Hiro.'

This time, it was Zelda's voice that interrupted. 'Yes, indeed, clone. You have my Master of Disguise in your space station–' she paused for effect '–but I have your Lieutenant Hiro in one of the ice caves. And there are hundreds. We will have to do business – won't we Doctor?'

Tiger knew that he had no option. It could take weeks to search the caves that dotted the ice-field. Weeks … and how long could any human survive in those temperatures?

'All right, Zelda. We'll make an exchange in the ice-field.' Lowering his voice to a whisper, he said, 'Maybe we can use a little deception of our own.'

Mary nodded. With Zelda, she thought, it was always better to have the upper hand. Her cubes could pull off all sorts of magical tricks. It would be important to arrive at the ice-field unannounced.

A freezing wind blew over the white wasteland of the ice-field, sending stinging particles rattling along the tundra. Hiro – the real Hiro – waited for his rescuers to arrive. There was no sign of anyone: no space craft, no thunder of engines. Nearby, a cube stood guard.

Zelda looked at Hiro and laughed her witchy laugh. 'It seems the despicable Ninestein has failed to keep the appointed hour,' she crowed. Hiro looked anxiously across the white plain, and strained his ears for the sound of engines.

'I'm here, Zelda.' Ninestein came round an outcrop of ice.

Zelda leapt backwards in surprise. 'I … I did not observe your arrival.'

'You weren't meant to,' Tiger snapped. 'Let's get this over.' Putting out an arm, the Terrahawks commander drew Moid from behind the ice-wall, and pushed him forward. He still resembled Hiro … but now it was a resemblance only. The face looked even more ashen and haggard. Moid's hand went to his face and he pulled away the mask that he had been wearing – the mask of Lieutenant Hiro's features. Beneath it was a horrifying, blank face. A nothing. Two deep pits for eyes. A slit for a mouth. White, empty, like the blank canvas of an artist before the paint is applied.

When he spoke, Moid's voice was blank too. 'I wear many faces,' he said, 'but have none of my own.' The words came out on a single, dreary note.

Ninestein and Hiro stared at Moid in horror; although there was something else in their eyes … something like pity.

'This is your creation, Zelda?' Ninestein asked in disgust. And even Zelda seemed to hang her head in shame. She had made this terrible being – this non-being – to serve her evil purposes. She had made someone who was no-one: something that was nothing, or worse than nothing.

Quickly, Zelda recovered herself. 'Moid,' she croaked. 'It is time to leave.' With one last pathetic stare at Tiger Ninestein, Moid followed his vile mistress towards her space craft. There came a blast of photon-drive, and they disappeared into the cold sky.

‘One can feel a certain sorrow – even for an enemy,’ remarked Hiro slowly, as the sound of the ship’s engines faded.

Ninestein was silent. *Yes,* he thought, *one can feel sorrow.* Not for Zelda – that would never be. But for the awful, tormented creature she had made. For the creature which could never be itself … but could *only* come alive when it was living behind another face.

‘Sure,’ he said. Then, ‘Let’s go.’

As he followed Tiger across the ice-field, Hiro looked around, still puzzled. Finally, he gave up.

‘How did you get here, Doctor?’

‘Well, I thought I’d drive the last few miles,’ Ninestein grinned.

Hiro’s confusion increased. ‘I can’t see anything.’

Ninestein’s grin broadened. ‘Hudson!’ he called. The Rolls-Royce seemed to grow out of the background, as it changed its colour from white to red.

Of course, Hiro realized, *I should have guessed it. After all – it was my own invention.* Hudson’s chameleon-like colouring had enabled the car to be perfectly camouflaged against the snow. An effect Zelda had not been prepared for. And, if she had had any little surprises planned, it had certainly nipped them in the bud.

Ninestein had been able to arrive on the scene silently – and invisibly.

Hiro and Tiger climbed into the car and settled back on the plush upholstery.

'I hope you were not too cold out there, Sir,' said Hudson, in his clipped accent. 'I did warn you about the possible thermal shock when leaving a controlled environment.' Was there something just a little boastful about the way Hudson used the word 'controlled'? Perhaps so.

Ninestein said: 'Yes you did, Hudson.'

'All part of the service, Sir,' came the response.

Balanced on a special perch at the front of the car, Zero had listened long enough to Hudson's boasting. It was time, he decided, to set matters straight. Surely Ninestein must have been joking – hadn't he? – when he suggested that 101 should get that medal. After all, who had been responsible for rousing the zeroids and spurring them into action? Who was it who had rallied his men – yes, *men* – with stirring talk of the regiment and tunes of glory? Who had been able to think that out for himself and touch the zeroids' true feelings?

'Sir,' he said eagerly, 'I'd like to talk to you about that medal.'

Tiger shot him a stern look. *'There are ways round that particular circuit.'* Wasn't that what he'd heard the sergeant-major say?

‘And I’d like to talk to you, Zero, about your truth circuit.’

Zero looked flustered. ‘Ah, yes sir. Well, what I said wasn’t true, of course. No … wait … I don’t mean it was a *lie.* No – I can't lie. That is to say – in a manner of speaking –’ His voice had become a rapid stammer of embarrassment.

‘Zero,’ said Tiger Ninestein. ‘Shut up!’ But there was the merest flicker of a smile on his face.

If You Have Enjoyed This Book….

If you enjoyed this book then keep a look out for upcoming releases of other Gerry Anderson screenplays, stories, and memorabilia taken from his personal archive.

You can keep up to date online via our websites and via social media:

The Official Gerry Anderson website:
www.gerryanderson.co.uk

Anderson Entertainment:
www.anderson-entertainment.co.uk

Facebook:
www.facebook.com/GerryAndersonOfficial

Twitter: @GerryAndersonTV

32454779R00089

Made in the USA
Charleston, SC
19 August 2014